To Be Honest

MAGGIE ANN MARTIN

Swoon READS

NEW YORK

To Be Honest

A SWOON READS BOOK

An imprint of Feiwel and Friends and Macmillan Publishing Group, LLC
175 Fifth Avenue, New York, NY 10010

Our books may be purchased in bulk for promotional, educational, or
business use. Please contact your local bookseller or the Macmillan
Corporate and Premium Sales Department at (800) 221-7945 ext. 5442
or by e-mail at MacmillanSpecialMarkets@macmillan.com.

Library of Congress Cataloging-in-Publication Data is available.
ISBN 978-1-250-18315-6 (hardcover) / ISBN 978-1-250-18474-0 (ebook)

Book design by Carol Ly

First edition, 2018

10 9 8 7 6 5 4 3 2 1

swoonreads.com

For my sister, Abbie.
This one's for you, kid.

chapter ONE

I'd never seen so much chevron in my life. We slowly unpacked all my sister's belongings in her small, dingy dorm room, and I wondered how it would ever feel homey. Right now it reminded me of a glorified prison cell with a set of worn-down loft beds and a free-standing sink in the corner. The cement floor was not helping in my sister's attempt to make the room prison-chic. Apparently they were redoing the floors and ran out of budget/time to put in new carpets for this year. Lucky Ash.

I helped her put the sheets on her loft bed (not an easy task, might I add) and we giggled as her corner boinked off and smacked her in the nose. Thank goodness for these moments when we could laugh, when we could forget what was going to happen in a few hours. Forget that I would be living without my sister and best friend for the first time in seventeen years.

No matter how many times Ashley tried to broach the

subject of her leaving this summer, I would always turn my head and plug my ears. I couldn't bear it then and suggested that we push off any sad or mushy conversations to the very last minute. I was a professional procrastinator in all things. Especially feelings.

"You put the bug liner on the mattress before the sheets, right, girls?" Mom asked, looking from a long list she'd printed out from one of her favorite mommy blogs.

"No bugs getting in this fortress," I said, smacking the bed. The force of my hand smack caused another corner of the fitted sheet to snap out from under the mattress, and Ashley scowled at me.

"I told you we should have gotten the extra-long sheets," Mom said.

"That's a waste of money. We had plenty of working twin sheets already," Ashley said. Always the practical one, she was. Ashley's brain was constantly in conservation mode while mom's brain was always in excess mode. Especially in the past two years, after Mom and Dad's divorce, Ashley has had to be the voice of reason in our home.

"The list said extra-long," Mom mumbled.

Ashley huffed after fixing the sheet once more, and we both climbed down from the loft. I offered to wind her twinkle lights around the base of the bed while she and Mom tag-teamed getting the minifridge up and running. Who knew you could have a teal minifridge with coral flowers? Only Ashley would upcycle our cousin's old, beaten-up minifridge to make it beautiful. She was going to film school, after all. It was kind of in her blood to be incredibly creative.

As Mom and Ashley exchanged a few heated words while trying to find an extension cord to keep the fridge in the "perfect feng shui location" of the room, I unwrapped the photos she packed. One was of her and me at summer camp the year that we were finally in the same cabin. We both slept in the bottom bunk that year because Ashley was afraid of heights and I was prone to falling out of the bed. I didn't mind, though. You can't quite explain the comfort of knowing your sister is close by.

The next was of our dog, correction, *her* dog, Fiyero. He earned his name during Ashley's obsession with the musical *Wicked*. Our family lived and breathed all things *Wicked* for the entirety of Ashley's eighth-grade year. The poodle baby in the picture looked like a stuffed teddy bear. Now Fiyero was a fifty-pound hellion who had a particular fondness for finding and eating makeup. I'd lost many a lipstick to the Fiyero monster.

The last picture was of Ashley, my dad, and me. We were in Hollywood doing a tour of Universal Studios because Ashley had just caught her movie bug. She was probably twelve, making me eleven. We posed in front of the *Gilmore*

Girls town of Stars Hollow and we were laughing our heads off. Most likely, Dad let out a fake fart noise right before the count of three, and we lost it. On the other side of the camera I could imagine Mom's disapproving face. Mom always refused to be in the pictures.

We worked in a scared silence, taking a few moments longer to complete each task than necessary. If we admitted that we were done, we'd have to admit that it was time to leave. I don't think Mom had good-bye on her epic list of dorm move-in responsibilities. No matter how many blogs she read or careful notes she took, nothing could prepare us for leaving.

"So when does your roommate get here?" I asked.

Ashley clapped her hands as the fridge hummed to life and she turned to me, taking the Universal Studios picture out of my hand.

"I think this afternoon. She lives in Kentucky, so it's a bit of a drive."

"Kentucky? They eat everything fried there, don't they? You'll have to be careful that you keep your healthy habits up while you're here," Mom said.

"I'm not sure that it's okay to generalize an entire group of people's eating habits based on a fast-food chain that happens to mention their state," I said.

"My metabolism hasn't changed in the last eighteen

years. I'll be fine, Mom," Ashley said. I envied the way that she could brush her off so quickly. Of course she could. Her entire life she'd been tall and slender, while I'd inherited the complete opposite body type.

Mom brought up a single finger, her telltale sign that you were about to get into an argument, but then she put it down. Almost like she remembered that we were here to drop off her oldest daughter for her freshman year of college and now wouldn't be the most convenient time for a fight.

"And she's bringing the futon?" she asked instead.

"I think she put one on hold at the Target nearby so she doesn't have to lug it up here with her. Don't worry, she sent me options and we mutually agreed on one," Ashley said.

"Because nothing can be left up to chance," I teased.

"There's nothing wrong with knowing how you like things," she said. "Plus, the first one she was looking at was way overpriced. I actually saved her a ton of money."

"I'll make sure to call you if I'm ever in the market for a futon," I said.

"You'll just use mine, silly," she said.

I sighed, twisting one of the bulbs that was winking out on the twinkle lights. "I was joking."

"Oh yeah, right," she said, grabbing on to her head. "Sorry. I'm all out of whack today. My funny-o-meter is broken."

"Only temporarily. It works best when you're settled and comfortable," I said.

"Will I ever be?" she asked. She finally took a moment to stop her hurried frenzy of setting things up to take in the room. Her breath became ragged, and I watched her eyes focus and unfocus. Seeing her panic in this way, seeing the mix of emotions racing through her, made my own stomach clench. We always joked that we were twins separated by almost twelve months, always in sync with each other in ways that were out of normal sister territory. Unfortunately, the months between our births robbed us of telepathy and the whole looking-alike thing. Physically, we are as opposite as it comes. She's tall and lanky with muddy-colored hair, where I'm short and chubby, my hair almost white it's so blond. About the only part that maybe hereditarily blessed both of us was bad eyesight. We can almost wear each other's prescription contacts.

I reached out to pull her into a very comforting (and comfortable) hug. We had the perfect builds for a great hug.

"Of course you will, honey," Mom said, joining our hug. She rested her cheek on the top of my head and we stayed this way for who knows how long until Ashley learned her first lesson about living in the dorms: If you wanted to have a private moment without someone bursting in to say hello, keep your door closed . . . and probably lock it, for good measure.

"Oh, yikes, I'm sorry," the girl at the door said. She had her hair pulled up in a messy bun that was leaning haphazardly to one side of her head. "I was just wondering if you had any extra duct tape that I could borrow? A cord on my microwave frayed. Don't tell the RA or whatever, because it might be a fire hazard, but I definitely don't have time or cash to get a new one. That's too much information. BLAH. Hi. My name is Yael."

"Hey," Ashley said, pulling away from our hug. "I'm Ashley. This is my little sister, Savannah, and my mom."

"Kim," Mom interjected.

"Nice to meet you all," Yael said. Her fingers tapped against the doorframe as she waited for something, anything to happen while we all stared at her. I turned to Ashley for a moment and tried to send her a telepathic "Grab the damn duct tape!" but she didn't catch my drift.

"Ash, you have some duct tape in the top drawer, right?" I asked, putting everyone out of their awkward misery.

"Oh! Yeah. Yes, I do," she said, breaking out of her stupor and grabbing the tape. She dropped it into Yael's open palm.

"You're seriously a lifesaver. See you around, Ashley," she said.

Ashley watched Yael skip down the hallway until I coughed to get her attention again. Ashley whipped around and started quickly unpacking more of her clothes. I smiled a little to myself. She thought Yael was cute.

"Well, are you both going to help?" she asked, her face still a light shade of red.

"We're all yours," Mom said. "I'll start folding sweaters. Savvy, can you load the sock and undies drawer? Do you need me to show you my sock-folding trick again?"

"I've got it under control," I said.

We worked in silence until every last bit of her clothes were meticulously placed in her closet and drawers. We rearranged the few knickknacks she'd allowed herself to bring and weighed the options of moving the fridge to the other side of the room at least three times. It was slowly reaching that point where we realized we were no longer needed in this dorm room, which meant an awful and painful good-bye was in my very near future.

"So," she said. "This is it."

"I guess so," Mom said. "Jeez, I'm glad they put water-proof mascara as a must-have on that list."

Mom pulled her into a bear hug, her head barely reaching Ashley's collarbone. Ashley leaned down to plant a kiss on her cheek and pulled away, wiping a stray tear from her cheek.

"I love you, Chicken," Mom said. "I think I just have to leave the room now before I become a complete mess. I'll meet you outside, Savvy, okay?"

I nodded, feeling the lump in my throat starting to block my airways. As Mom walked out of the room, both of our dissolves crumbled. We pulled each other into a tight hug, our bodies shaking as we cried. We'd never been apart for more than a week at a time, when she went to film camp a few summers in a row. Even those weeks were tough. I couldn't imagine *months* without her.

"We'll Skype all the time," she said. "We'll have sister check-ins throughout the day just like normal. The only thing that will change is that we won't be in the same room anymore."

"Is that supposed to make it better?" I said.

"I know things have been rough with you and Mom lately. Cut her a little slack, okay? She's gone through a lot of huge life changes this past year and is adjusting. I'll come home and visit as often as I can, but I won't be there anymore to be your buffer. Pick your battles, Savvy, okay?" she said.

I nodded. "I'll try to be better."

She held me by my shoulders and forced me to look into her eyes. "You're stronger than you know. Don't you ever forget that, no matter how tough things might get. And, it's not like I'm across the country. I'm only a few hours away if you ever need me."

I nodded again, curling into her for one last hug. When we pulled away it felt final. I felt like a part of me had been severed and I was leaving it behind. Like Cinderella's glass slipper, but if her leg was still attached. I decided that, like Mom, if I looked back again I would never leave. So I opened the door and closed it quickly behind me. I took my mom's hand and we walked down the hallway, down the flight of stairs, and to the car, where we cried for a good fifteen minutes before hitting the road again.

chapter TWO

I t had been exactly two days, thirteen hours, and thirty-four minutes since we left Ashley at Indiana State, and I was itching to get out of the house and away from my mom's sole attention. We'd already prepared healthy prep meals that we could freeze and eat for the next month, and if I had to dice one more carrot or make one more pot of rice, I would most definitely scream.

Thankfully, I'd already made plans with my best friend, Grace, to go to her family's summer cookout slash family field day in the park. Each year, the Morenos from around the Midwest came and joined for this day of fun (and sibling rivalry). I was mostly there for a chance to see her cousin Mateo . . . and hang out with Grace, of course.

Fiyero the poodle monster rested his chin on the side of my bed, rumbling a low, guttural growl, alerting me it was time to get up and play with him. I groaned as I rolled over and grabbed his fluffy face between my hands.

"Now that Ashley isn't here you have to resort to me, huh?" I asked.

Fiyero cocked his head like he was trying to understand me. His tongue, which was always a little too big for his mouth, flopped to the side and I barked out an early-morning laugh.

"You're lucky you're cute," I said.

As I stood up, Fiyero started bouncing around the room excitedly and then raced down the hallway and down the stairs. Much to my surprise, I heard Mom yelp "Fiyero!" from the bottom of the stairs. Usually Mom sleeps in until noon on the weekends, but today she was already up and stretching in the living room. Her hands contorted in weird angles behind her back and she listened to the soft hum of Lady Gaga, her workout music of choice.

"Want to join me and Fiyero on a run this morning?" she asked without turning around. My tiptoeing obviously failed me.

"As fun as that sounds . . ." I trailed off.

"The first step to a healthier life is making a commitment," she rattled off. I kept a mental tally of the thinspiration mantras she preached to me throughout the day. This one was at about two times a day.

"I inherited my commitment issues from Dad, obviously," I said.

I regretted saying it as soon as it came out. We tried not to talk about the Dad Debacle of Sophomore Year when he cheated on Mom with one of her friends. Should *friends* be in quotation marks in that context? Yes. Her "friend" slept with my dad for about a year before he slipped up, leaving his phone charging on the kitchen counter and leaving message previews open for a naive sophomore me to find. Adult sexting is disgusting.

"Oh, Savannah," she said, shaking her head with both of her hands firmly on her hips. It was a pose reserved for her times of greatest disappointment.

"Sorry, Mom," I said. "I have to head over to Grace's. She's having the Moreno family reunion thing this afternoon. Um, did you want to come, too?"

She shook her head. "No, thanks, sweetie. I'm heading over to the gym this afternoon. You have fun, though. Be sure to tell Maria thank you."

Her statement felt a little like a judgment. Like, *You have fun while I improve my mind, body, and spirit at the gym without you.* Most things out of her mouth sounded like a personal attack on me lately.

"I will. See you tonight," I said, heading into the kitchen.

"Do you want to heat up one of our frozen meals before you go? You don't need all the extra carbs that come with the grill-out food, especially the buns," she said.

My whole body flushed red like it did every time she tried to restrict my food. I remembered Ashley's plea to keep the peace while she was gone, and swallowed the anger that bubbled up inside of me.

"I'll be sure to heat one up before I leave, Mom," I lied. "Have fun at the gym."

Normally on Sunday mornings, Ashley would be up and making breakfast. She'd make secret pancakes and bacon before Mom could wake up and tell us how many calories we were wasting on breakfast. We'd lounge on the couch and watch episodes of whatever show we were binge-ing and practically become one with the couch before Mom woke up at noon. Maybe Mom woke up early so that I wouldn't feel so alone. Even though it made me feel a little better, the giant hole in our home dynamic expanded two sizes.

I listened to the soft rhythm of Mom's feet hitting the floor as she did her warm-up routine. I'd become accustomed to this sound over the past year. After Mom and Dad's divorce, Mom tailspinned into a shame spiral. She started making changes to every aspect of her life—anything to get her out of the "rut" she'd been in all those years with Dad. One night, she saw a call for audition tapes for the weight-loss reality TV show *Shake the Weight* and conned Ashley into helping her film a tape. Thinking nothing would come of it and being willing to do anything to make Mom happy in those months, Ashley helped her out.

About a month later, on Mother's Day, Mom got a call that she'd need to fly out to LA for a screen test with other potential contestants. Two weeks later, she was packing a bag to move out to LA and we were packing our bags to stay with Dad and Sheri for the next two months.

Each Wednesday night we would sit in front of the TV and watch this woman who was once our mother fight with other contestants, puke on camera, and shed a definitely unhealthy amount of weight in a few short months. She started praising the woman who barked orders at her, pushed her until she passed out, and caused her emotional damage she couldn't see happening to her. There is a reason people on these shows aren't allowed to call their family members while they're filming. Everyone would convince them to run from that place as fast as they could.

Now Mom inhabited a new, smaller body, after rigorous exercise and plastic surgery to remove some excess skin. I knew she was the same woman, could recognize her voice and her eyes, but everything else about her had changed. She had a one-track mind to count calories, follow to-do lists, and repeat the mantras that had been ingrained in her on *Shake the Weight*. She fixated not only on every little thing that crossed her lips but mine as well.

I snuck back up the stairs as Mom did arm circles to "Applause." The weather was sweltering. The Morenos always managed to host their family day on the stickiest day of the year. Thankfully, Mr. Moreno usually brought a sprinkler so that we could all cool down when it became unbearable.

The yellow-and-blue polka-dotted swimsuit sat snugly on my hips, and I instantly regretted opting out of swimsuit shopping this year. I figured I'd managed to squeeze into the same one for three years, what could possibly change in one more? Oh, right, everything. I flung on a T-shirt from Adventure World and slipped into my favorite flip-flops, on the verge of ripping in two. You can't beat a really nice pair of broken-in flip-flops.

When I came back downstairs, Mom and Fiyero had left for their run. I grabbed the keys to my new, inherited car. Ashley always had the touch with Norma (a very normal car name for a Nissan), but I absolutely despised driving. Thankfully Sandcastle Park was only a few-minutes drive away. If I could make it there with only a few bumps along the way, I would consider it a successful trip.

Sandcastle Park came into my view after a particularly violent curb check. I parked a block away and could still hear Mrs. Moreno greeting everyone as they showed up. She had the biggest heart, and the loudest voice to match. I once said that if I had to take one person with me on a deserted island, I'd take Mrs. Moreno because she could calm me down, cook some bomb food, and use her loud voice to track down civilization from miles away.

"Savannah! Savannah, over here, Savannah!" she called to me from across the street. I waved sheepishly as all of Grace's extended family turned to look at me.

"Hey, Mrs. M," I yelled back.

From the corner of my eye, I saw my best friend running my way. She wrapped me up in a hug, knocking the wind from me, in typical Grace fashion. When she pulled away, she held me by the shoulders and looked me up and down.

"How are you doing? Don't lie," she added, holding up an accusatory finger.

I sighed. "I've been better. But we're not here to have a pity party. We're here to have a fun day!"

"I signed us up for a three-legged race," she said, cringing as she waited for my response.

"You what?" I asked, knowing full well what I heard. Knowing full well that Grace knew that I refused to participate in this event every year since third grade, when I watched Andrew Adams break his leg while he was in a three-legged race with Cody Grant.

"You can't let the ghost of Andrew's broken-leg past haunt you forever. It's the only event I've never won. Come on, this is our *year*. I'll even get Mateo in on a conversation with you if that sweetens the deal," she said, wiggling her eyebrows.

"I feel really uncomfortable with you bribing me romantically with your family members," I said.

"Ugh, you wouldn't have cared if I didn't mention the three-legged race! What else do you want? I'll do anything," she said. When competitive Grace came out, you didn't want to get in her way. She wasn't above bribery if it meant she had the opportunity to win something.

"Do my laundry for the next month?" I offered.

"You know how much I despise laundry," she said.

"Take it or leave it, Moreno," I said.

She held out her hand for a binding handshake. "Deal."

After we shook, Grace took me on the grand tour of the attractions at this year's Moreno Family Field Day. First was a game of corn hole; next to it was a Slip 'N Slide and a rope for tug-of-war. One of the newer additions was a life-size chess board for a round of wizard's chess, spearheaded by Grace's little brother, Leo. For once in my life, I was grateful for Dad forcing Ashley and me to learn to play and go to chess club all those years ago. I was going to rock this wizard chess like it was nobody's business.

As I gazed over at the Slip 'N Slide, I saw a boy—no, a man—with luscious, wavy black hair and a smile that could melt the hearts of the iciest queens. Mateo had made the song "I Believe in a Thing Called Love" play in my head whenever I saw him since we were first introduced at the tender age of ten. We'd bonded over our matching Silly Bandz and it was pretty much love at first sight. For me, anyway. I was fully aware that sex gods like Mateo Moreno didn't look twice at girls like me.

"You can't just ogle my cousin while he's hanging out by a Slip 'N Slide." Grace laughed, elbowing me in the side.

"I'm actually ogling the Slip 'N Slide. Is that an extra ten feet at the end? Mrs. M went all out," I said.

"Sure," she said, rolling her eyes.

Mrs. M called everyone to gather around her picnic table to recite the rules for the day. No cheating would be tolerated, and Grandma Rosalina was the official ref. When I looked back to her she made "I'm watching you" fingers at me. Grandma Rosalina apparently didn't forget the year I ran into my competitors bumper-car style during the sack race. The second rule was to find your partner for the day. Under no circumstances were you to sabotage your partner during one-on-one activities to earn more points, or you would be disqualified. You'd think we were being filmed by ESPN with how strict they were about the rules.

"Now, pick your partners!" she yelled. Everyone frantically ran up to their desired partner, practically tackling other people out of the way to get to where they wanted to be. Grace and I instantly linked arms in a technique we'd perfected while having to find partners in school. Nothing could describe the sense of pure panic you felt when a teacher announced that you'd need a partner. Having the instant person you'd make eye contact with from across the room, sealing your partner bond, was the best feeling in the world.

"We're doing something a little bit more fun this year," Mrs. M announced. That sinking feeling that I just talked about? Yeah, let's multiply that by a thousand.

"You have to find a new partner! Everyone has been choosing the same ones for years and it's starting to get a little unfair. I'm looking at you, Roberto and Luis. Ready, set, find a new partner!" she said.

"Did you know about this?" I hissed to Grace.

"I had no idea!" she said.

We both frantically looked around for a new option, and I felt like we were competing in the Hunger Games. Or, I felt like I was going to get picked last like in gym class. I think both scenarios are equally terrifying. Everyone was pairing off, hurtling their bodies at each other in what seemed like slow motion in my mind. I whipped my head around, and my eyes locked on Mateo from across the park. He started to lift his hand up to wave at me, the most iconic symbol of "Let me be your partner" in the universe, before Leo snatched his hand and claimed him as his partner. Damn it, Leo, now I'm really going to have to own you in wizard's chess.

"Who's left?" Mrs. M yelled from her picnic table. Everyone looked around and stared at each other. Really? Just me then?

"I'm super alone, Mrs. M," I said, which garnered a few pity laughs from the crowd. It got quiet for a moment before one more person spoke up from the back.

"Also super alone," said a male voice that I didn't recognize. He stepped out from behind a cluster of people and into my vision. He didn't look like the majority of the Morenos— he was unbelievably tall, with strawberry blond hair. He was at least the height of two Grandma Rosalinas combined. He inhabited that awkward in-between boy stage where they lacked muscle definition but their forms had outgrown their younger bodies.

"Great! Savannah, you will be with George. Now, everyone, it's time to start with the egg toss! We'll go in waves of five. Everyone come on over to the other side of the park so we can start," Mrs. M said.

While everyone started walking toward the other side of the park, I walked in the opposite direction to meet George. My palms started to sweat and my heart fluttered in my chest the way it tends to when I meet new people for the first time. It didn't help that he had some exceptionally dreamy brown eyes that crinkled in the corners when he smiled. I wonder what it said about me that I found my best friend's extended family attractive.

"Hey," I said, waving a little. "I'm Savannah."

"George," he said, holding out his hand. It made me feel a little better that his hands were shaking, too.

"Are you . . . Grace's cousin? Friend of the family?" I asked.

I meant it innocently, since I obviously fell under the "family friend" category, but his face turned down. "I know I don't look traditionally Colombian, but I'm a Moreno."

"Oh! Oh shit, no, that's not what I meant. Seriously, I just, I'd never seen you before and I honestly didn't know," I said, wanting to kick myself for being so inconsiderate.

"I mean, I'm not technically a Moreno, like, my last name is Smith, which now seems like it's defeating the point. My mom's Colombian. My dad's very Irish. Hence the hair," he said.

"Okay, cool. Well, I'm Savannah Alverson, with a painfully uninteresting cultural background. I think my dad has some strong Norwegian ties in his family, but I can't be sure," I said.

We stared at each other for a few solid seconds, taking in each other's cultural history, before Mrs. M's voice sounded again.

"We're about to start! Savannah! George! Get a move on!" she said.

That was our cue to speed-walk over to the rest of the group. The egg toss was my peak event each year. I'd perfected my soft-palmed catch down to a science and knew how to arc the egg perfectly so that my partner could catch it without a problem. I tried my best to divulge all my techniques to George as we joined the rest of the family on the other side of the park.

"You see, I have a bit of a reputation to uphold," I said. "I've been dubbed egg master for the past three years. And I'm not prepared to revoke my title today."

"Teach me your ways," George said, with a lopsided smile.

"The key is to imagine where the egg is going to land before it even leaves your hand. I think positive affirmation works wonders. If you think the egg will land softly in your partner's hand, it will," I said.

"Okay, Mr. Miyagi."

I grabbed an egg from Mrs. M's hand and George and I met in the middle with all the other teams. Mrs. M instructed each of us to take four steps back from our partners to start the game. I caught the wave of Mateo's luscious hair out of the corner of my eye, and turned to take one last peek before I entered competition mode.

"Good luck, Savvy." Mateo smiled.

Normally I would say something like "You know I don't need luck" or "I'm the one who should be wishing *you* luck," but the sparkle of Mateo's eyes in the sun made my mind completely incapable of forming a coherent comeback.

"Uh, yeah, you too," I said.

"Savannah!" George yelled at me from across the park. My head snapped back to him and he mouthed "Focus!" while attempting a tree yoga pose. Which did not make me focus more, for the record. It made me snort out an entirely unattractive laugh that Mateo definitely heard.

"On your marks, get set, toss!" Mrs. M yelled.

The egg left my hands with the perfect arc and velocity to land peacefully in George's hand without too much difficulty on his end. I held my breath as it made contact, and he held it up, intact, with a surprised look on his face. I sent him an encouraging thumbs-up before he sent the egg back my way.

We took another four steps back away from each other. This was usually the round where people started cracking their eggs or dropping them. You could hear a mix of shrieks and "Are you kidding me?"s as we kept progressing through the rounds. And then, there were three groups left. It was getting harder and harder to see the egg flying through the air, and I thought for sure he would not catch it as I tossed it across the park. But, by some stroke of egg-god luck, we were the last ones standing as the other two groups dropped theirs.

"Our egg toss champion wins again!" Mrs. M yelled.

George gave me a giddy high five that made me giggle. I'd never seen anyone as excited as me about an egg toss. He carried that same enthusiasm as we competed in the ring toss, only coming in third place for that activity. It was harder for me to aim the rings to get on the tiny post than it was to pass an egg to my partner, for some reason.

Next, we separated for our first individual event of balloon archery. And even though I didn't make it into the top five finalists, I felt accomplished that none of my arrows went astray and threatened anyone's life this year. It took a lot of trust and reassurance on my part to earn my bow and arrow back in the past few years. Mrs. M would hardly forget the time that a stray arrow of mine knocked over the cake that she'd been working on the whole day before.

I was about to tell George the story about my faulty arrow when Mrs. M's voice boomed over the crowd.

"All right, now it's time for the three-legged race. We're going to go in waves of five and do it bracket-style. Come to me to grab your team's rope and get prepared," Mrs. M said.

George volunteered to go get our rope for the three-legged race, and I watched him run away in his basketball shorts. Grace sat on the ground, joining her leg with one of her younger cousins. I suddenly felt self-conscious about the short shorts I chose to wear over my swimsuit. Imagining my jiggling thigh having to be tied up to a stranger's was my version of a nightmare. Would he notice the stretch marks that striped down my inner thighs? Would he be disgusted by me when he saw them?

"What's the best way to tie two legs together?" George asked. "I figured you must be a pro at this, too."

I could barely understand what he said as my brain started to shut down at the thought of tying my leg to George's.

"Um, yeah, this is the first time I'll be doing this event," I said.

He shook his head, completely oblivious to my internal freak-out. "Cool. So it will be a learning experience for both of us. Do you want to take this end and wrap it around your thigh and I'll pull this end through mine? Then we can try a loop knot. I think that will be the most comfortable. What do you think? Savannah?"

It suddenly felt like all the air had been pushed out of my lungs. I swayed on my feet as the ringing in my ears began. No matter how many panic attacks I had, my body always believed that it was dying. My body told me that I couldn't catch my breath, that I was going to actually die in

Sandcastle Park in my polka-dotted swimsuit before I even got to eat lunch.

I plopped onto the ground and put my head between my legs, trying to catch my breath again. George's voice played over the pounding of my heart and the ringing in my ears, but I couldn't understand what he was saying. I squinted my eyes closed in an effort to make everything stop. My body didn't listen. I felt someone move my ponytail from off my neck and offer me a bottle of water. When I could finally look up, Grace's eyes met mine. Grace. Thank God for her.

"Hey, bud," she said. "I never should have pushed you to do the three-legged race. I know how much it freaks you out, and I should have respected your limits."

"S'okay," I whispered, my bottom lip shaking involuntarily.

"Are you breathing? Do you want my phone so you can use my meditation app?" she asked.

"I'm okay; I'll be fine," I said. My body was starting to believe me now, too. Calming down from a panic attack felt like you had run a marathon. When your body freaks itself out so thoroughly that adrenaline pumps through you and all your muscles become tight at the same time, it can seriously kick your ass.

"Do you want me to drive you home?" she asked.

"I can do it," George interjected. "I know Lizzie really wants to race. I'll make sure she gets home."

Grace cocked her head at me, gauging my comfort level. My eyes slid to little Lizzie tapping her feet on the ground, the rope still tied around her thigh. I couldn't ruin an adorable seven-year-old's afternoon with my seventeen-year-old meltdown.

"That would be nice," I managed to get out. Grace rubbed her hand up and down my arm while whispering a quick thank-you to George. Lizzie clapped as Grace returned and tied their legs together effortlessly. The rope had more than enough give between them and Grace's perfect, toned legs would never get chafed by the rope.

George held out his hand to help me up. I put all my focus into getting my legs to move again without wobbling. They only felt a little bit like Jell-O by the time I was fully standing, and I could walk around without feeling like I could faint any second.

"I'm going to pull my car up to the curb here. Are you okay to wait for a second while I go grab the keys from my mom?" he asked.

"Go ahead," I said. Everything was a bit of a blur when he ran back to grab the keys and bring the car around. I tried to focus on the moving leaves of the tree directly in front of me. Anything to distract me from the way my lungs seized up every few seconds, threatening to send me spiraling again. The leaves followed a pattern as the wind gusted underneath them. Slow left, slow right, quick up. Slow left, slow right, quick up.

"Savannah!" George yelled from the car as he idled by the curb.

My eyes readjusted to take in the black Suburban in front of me. I shuffled my way there, opening the passenger door as quickly as I could manage so that I could flop into the seat. I slid the seat belt across my body and felt his eyes on me. I knew he was concerned, but it wasn't helping with how self-conscious I was already feeling.

"Where do you live?" he asked, pulling out his phone to put it in his GPS.

"Nine Ninety-Two Mulberry Court," I managed. A British voice erupted from the car's speakers instructing George how to get back to my place. We sat in silence only broken by the occasional "Turn left in seventy feet. Recalculating. Turn right in thirty feet."

This was the single most embarrassing moment of my life. I was letting a stranger drive me back home after I had a panic attack with just the thought of participating in a children's picnic game. He had to think I was the biggest loser in the world.

"How are you feeling?" We were a few seconds from

pulling into my driveway, and I just wanted to melt with humiliation into my seat.

"I'm doing better," I said. "I'm sorry that you had to leave because of me."

"Ah, don't worry about it," he said. "I think I used up all my luck on that egg toss. Every other competition would have been disappointing in comparison."

My smile quivered, and I felt like I might break out into full-blown panic again if I didn't get out of the car. Now. I could not do this in front of him again.

"Thanks again," I said, reaching for my door handle, very aware of how heavily my hands were shaking.

"Do you need me to stay with you for a second?" he asked.

"Oh, gosh no, you've already done enough," I said. I opened the door with a shaking hand and managed to wiggle myself out of the tall car.

"It's really no big deal, I can stay—" he started.

"I don't need you to stay with me, okay? I'm perfectly fine without your help," I snapped.

He shook his head the smallest bit as I slammed the door shut. I marched to the front door of my house and into the front room. I collapsed onto the couch and let my body properly process the anxiety and sadness I'd bottled up in the last few days. Jagged breaths came in between my tears that I'd worked so hard to keep at bay. My loneliness was truly starting to sink in. I couldn't run up the stairs and get a hug from my sister. I couldn't tell her about my panic attack—she wouldn't be able to analyze it for what it really was.

This year was a new, huge, exciting adventure for Ashley. I'd never felt more abandoned.

chapter THREE

First days of school are always made out to be this momentous occasion full of school-spirited montages. In reality, it goes on like any other day, only the parking lot is generally more of a disaster as the sophomores who now have parking spots try to navigate it for the first time. I usually parked Norma as far on the outskirts of the lot to avoid the mess. I looped my book bag over my shoulders and headed inside, barely dodging a driver who was racing to get a close spot. I yelped, jumping back, and waited for the person to come out of the car so I could give them an earful.

"Did you even see me there? You almost hit me!" I yelled.

"Oh my God, I'm so sorry," said a very familiar voice. As he climbed out of his car, his look of panic turned into a frown.

"Since when do you go here?" I asked George.

He slung his bag across one shoulder and started to walk

toward the front door. I barely kept up with him, my short legs working double just to keep up with his long stride.

"I transferred this year," he said.

"Why would you transfer for your senior year?" I asked.

"Junior," he replied.

"That explains the driving," I replied.

He shot me a sideways glance before shaking his head in the same fashion as he had dropping me off at my house yesterday. We started down the hallway, and I smiled at a few people as we walked by. They all looked quizzically at George as he passed. We made it almost down to the cafeteria, near where my locker was, before we ran into Grace.

"Hey, you two! What a fun surprise," Grace said, enveloping me in a hug. She pulled George into a hug, too, and he awkwardly patted her back.

"Can you actually show me where the office is?" George asked Grace.

"I could have shown you," I said.

"I'm perfectly fine without your help," he repeated back at me. The words that I'd spat out at him in my moment of panic stung when they were thrown back in my face. Grace's mouth fell open, and she looked between us for a few seconds.

"Fine. Have a super first day," I said. I turned on my heel and started to walk the opposite way down the hallway, away from my locker, with no destination in mind. The stinging of tears and the lump in my throat started to creep up, and I looked everywhere for the nearest bathroom. I refused to be the girl crying in the hallway on the first day of school.

The girls' restroom at the end of the hall came into view, and I started to speed-walk in that direction. But, the universe had a fun way of interrupting me when I was on a mission.

"Savannah!" I heard from the doorway of a classroom. I turned around slowly to take in a waving Mrs. Brandt, who cradled a cup of coffee in her hands. At least some things stayed consistent from year to year. She waved me over to talk to her, and I cursed internally.

"I see you're not signed up for newspaper this year. You're going to leave me hanging without one of my best reporters?" she asked.

"I'm sorry, Mrs. Brandt," I said. Genuinely, it was a tough decision to not take newspaper this year. It was between newspaper and AP chem, which I needed to get into the engineering program at Indiana State. Ever since Ashley decided that she was going to Indiana State, I found out the requirements for getting into my program and was doing everything in my power to make that happen. "I couldn't fit it into my schedule this semester."

"Who's your counselor?" she asked, leading me inside to

her desk. She scrounged around through two overstuffed drawers and on through a filing cabinet until she found a scrap of paper to write on.

"Mr. Reed," I said.

She scribbled a few notes down on the slip of paper before handing it to me. "Go talk to Mr. Reed and see if you can start an independent study for newspaper. I can meet with you after school to collaborate on story ideas. I understand if you have too much on your plate. Just think about it. I hate to see you give up something that you're so great at."

As I went to grab the paper, Mrs. Brandt really looked me in the eyes for the first time in her frenzy. Her face immediately turned to concern.

"Is everything all right?" she asked. "I'm sorry if I overwhelmed you."

"No, no, it's not you," I said, wiping under my eyes to catch some spillover tears. The warning bell rang, signaling that I had five minutes to make it to my first class of my senior year. Students started to roll into Mrs. Brandt's classroom, and I took this as my cue to leave. "I'd better get to class. I'll talk to Mr. Reed."

"Ah—okay, talk to you soon," she shouted after me as I dodged my way through a sea of students. I moved through them like an emotionless zombie, my usual resolve during difficult or painful days taking hold. I never cried in front of people who weren't Ashley. It was like not having her as an emotional buffer was opening the floodgates to all emotional interactions with people. I was not a fan of this change, to say the least.

I spotted Grace, alone this time, on the other side of the hallway. Her eyes widened when she saw me, and we rushed to reach each other.

"I see you and George have already started World War Three," she said.

"I *might* have accidentally started it. But to be fair, he did almost run me over in the parking lot this morning," I replied.

"Because he was mad at you?" she asked.

"No! On accident. But I *might* have given him some crap for it," I said.

"Of course you did," she said, rolling her eyes and smirking. We walked together to our first-period class. "Remind me again why I agreed to eight thirty calc?"

"Because this is the only one that fit into my schedule and you wanted to have full access to my notes," I said. I linked my arm with hers. "And because you love me."

"This is really testing my love right now," she said.

"So Mrs. Brandt wants me to do an independent study for the paper," I said, sliding into a desk in our calculus room. Grace's eyes went wide and she clapped excitedly.

"Tell me you're going to do it. We can work on a big investigative story like we've talked about for years! Come on, you'll be the best partner ever because you already appreciate all my character quirks. Please, Savvy, please do this!" she said.

"I'll think about it," I said, playing around with the sheet of paper that Mrs. Brandt had given me. The warning bell rang, and more of our classmates filled in the chairs around us. Our teacher, Mr. Kavach, went to the front of the room and started rattling off attendance and the nerdy school-loving part of my brain got excited.

Even with my morning brain, calculus came easy to me. It gave me a chance to use everything I'd learned before, all the ideas from algebra and geometry that I'd taken the time to memorize, and build upon them. It let me solve things in a perfect world, where the only things that mattered lived on the page. I could decide how to get to the answer. I had the freedom to find my own path. Also, Mr. Kavach was pretty cool, which helped.

Grace scribbled down notes idly next to me, which were probably more like doodles. She knew that I took great calc notes and we would study together eventually. The class drew to a close, and Grace packed up her things quickly.

"I've got to go meet Ben out by his locker, but I'm honestly begging you to do the independent study with me.

You're such a great writer, Sav, the paper needs some hard-hitting reporters this semester," she said.

Ben was Grace's newly minted boyfriend. They worked at Famous Footwear together over the summer, and a relationship blossomed among the surrounding sneakers and Ugg boots. I was still a little weary of Grace dating a jock, but he seemed nice enough from the few times that I'd met him.

"I'll seriously think about it," I said.

"You better!" she said, blowing me a kiss as she walked down the hallway. "See you at lunch!"

After school I picked up a happy Fiyero from the groomer, his fur looking clean for the first time in weeks. I guess that's the risk you take adopting a white puffball of a dog. He's pristine for a few hours before he rolls in something he shouldn't. Fiyero frowned at me as I buckled him into his harness in the back seat and then I imagine had thoughts of panic when he realized I was driving. Animals are very attuned to imminent danger.

Norma pulled through once again and delivered us home with only minor psychological trauma, mostly on Fiyero's part. I apologized to him profusely for almost knocking him over after a particularly sharp right turn. He dashed out of the car once I opened the door and jumped into the arms of my mother, who was home from work. She already had her too-tight bike pants and sports bra on. It was an effort to show off her transformation to the neighbors, like they all didn't notice her new body already.

"How was your first day?" she asked as Fiyero licked a giant, slobbery kiss onto the side of her face.

"It was fine," I said. "Is it possible for senioritis to already be kicking in?"

"Oh, come on, you love school!" she said. "You're so smart, Savannah Lynn. Don't let the concept of a senior slack year throw you off from your trajectory."

"Don't worry about me, Mom," I said. Normally, I'd add something like "You haven't much in the past," but Ashley's advice on picking my battles rose to mind. If we were going to make our cohabitation without Ashley work, I'd have to work on the whole "processing what I was going to say before blurting it out" thing.

We walked through the door and Fiyero immediately went to his container of treats, as if he deserved a treat for surviving the car ride with me. I couldn't really argue with his logic. He sat patiently as I grabbed one of the smelly bones from the smelly container and set it down in front of him. I was about to head upstairs and start on my homework (after one deserved episode of *Buffy*, of course), when Mom called my name.

"Savannah, come back down here for a second," she said.

Nothing good ever started with that sentence.

"As you know, it's almost been six months since my time on *Shake the Weight*," she said when I reached the foot of the stairs. "They are getting ready to film their check-in special and want to come by the house next week to get some footage. It will be mostly of me doing things in my everyday life. They might ask to interview you about how things have changed. You know, just basic things."

"Are you having Ashley come home for it?" I asked.

"Oh, no, sweetie. She needs to adjust to her schedule at school. Coming back only two weeks in would mess up the routine she's establishing. You wouldn't want to set her back, would you?" she asked.

"Definitely not," I replied. My gut lurched. Having to go on camera and speak positively about my mom's transformation sounded like a nightmare. Not only did I disagree with everything the show stood for, but a smaller, more vicious part of my subconscious believed that they'd ask if I was interested in being on their teen *Shake the Weight* show. I couldn't handle someone asking me that.

"You don't seem very excited," she said, frowning. "It will be great for our community to be featured again."

"You know how I feel about this show, Mom," I said.

She sucked in her cheeks before putting her hand to her forehead. "Why is it always such a battle with you to ask for your support?"

"I support *you*. I don't support the show," I said.

"I am me because of that show, don't you get it? I was no one before it. Now I'm someone. I can finally be my true self. Isn't that something worth celebrating?" she asked.

"You were someone to me," I said quietly. We sat in a few beats of silence before she turned her back on me, heading into the living room.

"Can I at least ask you to fake it? Smile pretty for the cameras when they come?" she asked.

"Whatever," I said, continuing the journey upstairs to my room. The only person who would understand and support my decision to fight back in this moment wasn't here, but I needed to hear her voice. And I had a feeling she needed to hear mine right about now, too.

The phone rang twice before Ashley answered on the other end of the line.

"Hi, cutie," she said when she answered.

"It's so good to hear your voice," I said. "How was your first day of classes? Did you make any friends? Enemies? *Frenemies?*"

She laughed. "My roommate moved in! She's pretty

great. And I ended up having a few classes with the girl Yael from down the hall. Only time will tell if we become frenemies."

"I have a feeling Yael will *not* be a frenemy," I said.

"Stop, we don't even know yet if she's interested in me," she said.

Oh, Ashley, always the practical one, never the dreamer.

"I'm just saying, she was super cute," I said.

"Enough about me. What about you? How was your first day?" she asked.

"I almost got run over by Grace's cousin. I think I've started a feud with him. Still unclear at this point," I said.

"See? You have enough frenemies for the both of us," she said.

I twirled a piece of my hair around my finger so tightly that it started to turn blue. I tried to figure out the best way to break the news that Mom and I had our first big fight sans Ashley. There was no good way to start.

"So," I started. "*Shake the Weight* is coming to film some check-in footage of Mom next week."

After a long pause, "Oh," was all she could say.

"Just when you think you've exorcised the demons," I said.

"Does she want me to come back home?" she asked.

"Oh, gosh no!" I said. "You stay put. You're still getting

used to things. I have to at least give you some time to make a frenemy before you can come back for a visit."

"You're sure you don't want me to come back home?" she asked.

Of course I did. I wanted more than anything for her to come back and be the sister who does all the talking on camera. I wanted her to be in the footage, with Mom and Fiyero in the background. No one would judge her for being the fat daughter who didn't follow her mom's advice she learned from *Shake the Weight*. No one would question her.

"I'm positive. I've got this," I said.

"I told you you're stronger than you think," she said. "I'm proud of you, Sissy. Things are going to be okay with us separated, you know? It's just something we'll have to get used to."

"At least for this year. And then I'll come join you and we can be roommates and go back to normal," I said.

She paused on the other end of the line again. "You're sure you want to come here? You're one of the smartest people I know—you can probably get in somewhere even better than here."

"Of course I'm sure!" I said. "This is only temporary. As long as I know that this is only temporary, I feel much better about everything."

"Whatever you say," she said. I could almost imagine her

shaking her head in her dorm room. I heard the sound of a door slamming, and Ashley said a quick hello to her roommate.

"Isabel is back. Can I call you tomorrow?" she asked.

"Sounds good," I said. "Do you want to start season two of *Scandal* tonight? We could text throughout however many episodes as we can stay awake for?"

"You know it," she said. "I have to support my girl Olivia Pope."

"Good. As long as we both express our mutual love for OP over text message, then all is right with the world," I said. "I miss your face so much already."

"I miss your face more. Talk to you later, 'kay?"

" 'Kay. Bye, Sissy," I said. The line cut abruptly on the other end before she could echo back her typical "Bye to you, too, Sissy." I looked at the phone in my hand for a few seconds, waiting to see if she'd call back to correct her mistake. The phone stayed silent in my hand, and I flopped onto my bed, letting out a long sigh.

Week one without Ashley: 1. Savannah: 0.

chapter FOUR

Not a few seconds after I reached my locker, I felt Grace's presence behind me. She had one of those energies that you just felt whenever she was around, like a warm hug without her even touching you. Her calc book rested on her hip, and she looked at me expectantly, like she had something on the tip of her tongue that she was dying to spit out.

"I have the best idea for our story," she said.

"You know I haven't officially signed up for the independent study, right?" I asked.

She waved her hand in front of her face. "I know you will. You can't pass up a good story."

"Dazzle me," I said, picking up my calc book out of my locker. I slammed it shut and turned to walk to class with her. Grace excitedly pitching a story was probably 85 percent why she was voted editor of the school paper this year. Her love of journalism was infectious.

"So I was talking to Melinda Aldridge this morning, and

she mentioned that the dance team was trying to practice in the gymnasium yesterday afternoon, but the boy's *baseball team*, which doesn't even start until spring, had somehow reserved it. But the dance team had never had to reserve the space before," she said.

"You're kidding," I said, actually getting kind of into it.

"Right? Anyway, they were kicked out and forced to practice in the cafeteria, with not enough space and horrible acoustics, when they have a performance this weekend at the football game. How unfair is that? It got me thinking about the disparities between boys' and girls' sports and how the school shows its favoritism. Like, letting the baseball guys reserve a space that had always been the dance team's. I'm thinking there might be some favoritism in funding, too. That's why I would want Mrs. Brandt as our faculty instructor. If we find some dirt that the school wouldn't want us to publish, we need her to have our back legally."

"Whoa," I said.

"If we can prove it, we could totally make some changes in our own school. We could make a difference," she said.

We both slid into our seats in calc, and I was suddenly jazzed to have a project to work on. I was already scheming up ways to get interviews with the athletes of the school, even some of the coaches, without telling them exactly what the story was about. I'd ask them about practices, where they usually practice, the process they go through to get those facilities—it wouldn't be too hard to get some foundational dirt.

Mr. Kavach started the class by announcing a quiz for Friday. Not really the first thing that people want to hear at eight thirty on a Tuesday. Grace looked over to me with wide eyes and mouthed, "Help me." I mouthed back a confident "I got you." At least I hoped I did. I would have to go home tonight and study so that I could help Grace study the rest of the week.

After class was finished, Grace and I both rushed into the hallway, trying to beat the crowds, to head to our next class.

"So is it safe to say we're having a calc study session on Thursday?" she asked.

"Totally," I said. "And maybe tomorrow we can get started on the story?"

"Tomorrow?" she said, her voice reaching a new octave. "Uh, tomorrow after school I have plans. I'm, uh, going to hang out with Grandma Rosalina. She needs help setting up for a party she's throwing."

"On a Wednesday?" I asked.

"The elderly don't party on our same schedule," she said.

"You're allowed to say that you're hanging out with Ben, Grace. He is your boyfriend," I said.

"I know, I just know that we've always promised each other that we'd never become those girls who forget about their best friends the moment they get boyfriends, and I don't want to be that person; I really don't," she said.

The only thing that saved her from further questioning was the warning bell for my second-period class. I had been given a very specific warning from our gym teacher that if I was late for class this year he wouldn't be as lenient with all my excuses like last year.

"I have to go to gym, but you don't have to lie to me about hanging out with him. It's very okay!" I said.

She mouthed "Thank you" to me as she continued down the hallway to her second-period class.

I made it halfway to the gymnasium before I realized that I'd left my phone on my seat in Mr. Kavach's room. I weaved in and out of the kids texting and taking up more general hallway width than necessary to talk to their group of friends. If I didn't hurry, I'd for sure be late and get points off for gym.

When I walked back into Kavach's room, he and George were talking. My body heated with a mixture of embarrassment and anger. As if he could feel me looking his way, he turned around to face me but quickly turned back to Mr. Kavach. Like he could pretend he didn't see me, when we so clearly made eye contact. I huffed and started to go up the aisle, where my phone would be sitting in my seat. To my dismay, it was nowhere to be seen. Dang. It.

"Savannah," Mr. Kavach said. As I flipped around to look at him, he waved my phone in his hands.

"Oh, thank God," I said.

"Savannah, have you met George yet?" Kavach asked. "He's new this year. A junior taking precalc."

"Yeah, we've——" I started as George simultaneously stuck out his hand for a handshake.

"Nice to meet you," he said.

I shook my head in disbelief but took his hand. What exactly was his damage?

"It's funny, George, you have a very familiar face," I said back. "I'd better head back to gym. I'm going to be late."

I smiled a tight smile and turned on my heel, my blood boiling.

"I was just suggesting that you would be a great peer tutor for George. His old school didn't offer up as much of the calc foundation in other math courses like we did, so he's a little behind because of it," he said.

It was George's turn to turn bright red. Good.

"Oh, I don't know——" I started.

"Think about it, Savannah. Maybe you two could swap numbers if you decide you have the time. I know it would be a big help to George."

I looked to George, who had refused to meet my eyes during this entire conversation. Truthfully, I just need him to say one word, one phrase that indicated that he actually needed and wanted my help. I wouldn't mind it—precalc was arguably one of my favorite classes. I raised an eyebrow and tilted my head, as if I was waiting for him to say that he'd be interested.

"Um, yeah, sure let's swap numbers," he said.

"Great. Thanks, Savannah. See you fifth period, George," Mr. Kavach said. George threw his backpack over one shoulder, and I started making my way to the door.

"Okay, let's walk and talk. I'm seriously going to be docked points if I don't get to gym soon," I said. The hallways were thinning out, meaning it was almost time for the second-period bell to ring. Teachers were starting to shut their doors behind them, and the noise of slamming doors reverberated off our emerald-green lockers. Once we were out of Kavach's earshot and in the hallway, I whipped around to face him.

"What the heck was that? Why did you pretend not to know me back there?" I demanded.

"What was I supposed to say, 'Yeah, we've met—I pissed her off yesterday morning when I almost turned her into a car pancake'?" he asked.

"Or something like, 'Yeah, I'm her best friend's cousin'? Even a nice 'Yep, we totally have' would have cut it. Seriously, are you that embarrassed to say that you know me? Kavach is, like, the last person you need to seem extra cool around. He's very much in the Savannah fan club," I said.

The redness in his face had reached the tops of his ears and he wrapped a hand around the back of his neck. He looked up and down the hallway before turning back to me.

"I panicked, okay? I had a feeling that he was going to offer you up as a tutor, and I was embarrassed that you'd know I was bad at math. Happy now?" he said. He was bright red all over. His fair complexion had become an entire shade that matched his embarrassment, and my gut wrenched. I'd made him feel this way.

"George——" I started. The second-period bell cut me off.

"I have to get to band," he said. He walked down the opposite hallway from me, and I stood there, a doofus without a hall pass who was now officially late for gym.

"I'll catch you later!" I said. He didn't look back or answer me.

———

When I got home, the overwhelming smell of Mom's signature kale and ginger smoothies struck me like a smack in the face, and I gagged. I put my shirt over my nose in an effort to smell the laundry detergent on my blouse instead of the ginger that seemed to be seeping into my nostrils anyway. I walked into our open-concept kitchen to find Mom by her blender with enough kale to take up all the counter space plus our kitchen island.

"Was there a really good deal on kale at the store?" I asked, plugging my nose as I talked so that everything came out with a nasally tone.

"I'm going on a juice cleanse," Mom said with a smile plastered on her face. "I have to drop ten pounds before *Shake the Weight* comes to film, and Lindsay recommended this kale juice cleanse that she went on a few weeks ago."

Lindsay was another contestant who was on *Shake the Weight* with Mom. She lived in suburban Iowa, so she and Mom really bonded while they were on the show together. Mom always rubbed it in my face that Lindsay's family had taken on her healthy eating habits without any protest and that they'd collectively lost one hundred fifty pounds. I usually responded with something like "Good for Lindsay's family" or "Sorry we're not interested in joining your health cult," neither of which usually went over well.

"Well, that sounds fun," I said. "While you blend up your meals for the next week, I'm going upstairs to go work on homework."

I turned to go, but she called out to me.

"Savannah, wait!" she said. Part of me wanted her to admit how unhealthy it was to go on this juice cleanse, or that she didn't really need to drop the ten pounds before the crew came to our house. But that was just the wishful-thinking side of me.

"I have to post a picture of myself with this protein powder that is sponsoring me on Instagram. Can you take the photo for me?" she asked.

"Couldn't you get someone at work to help you with this?" I asked. "You work at a PR firm. It's literally your coworkers' jobs to do this kind of stuff."

She rested her hands on her hips and gave me the Look of Disappointment before I finally caved.

"Fine. Where do you want me to take it?" I asked.

Mom poured herself an Insta-worthy green kale juice in one of our fanciest glasses and brought out her copper measuring cups and her cooking knife to arrange on the table in front of her. She held up her kale juice and positioned the protein powder to be in the top right corner of the photo with her smiling in the background. She wore one of her smallest neon pink sports bras that showed off the most of her new body, and she made me count down when I was taking the picture so that she could simultaneously suck in her stomach and squeeze her muscles at the same time. All tricks that she had learned while she had to take photos on the show.

"Do you mind writing the caption for me? You're so

much quicker than I am at writing things out on the phone," she said.

I almost protested, but she started rattling off the caption before I could say no.

" 'Enjoying a refreshing kale juice infused with Power Powder'—make sure to use that little trademark thingy—'this afternoon. I'm starting a juice cleanse this week and need some accountability buddies. Who's with me? Leave me your messages of encouragement in the comments. Love you all! Hashtag healthy life, hashtag inspiration, hashtag *Shake the Weight*, hashtag weight loss, hashtag juice cleanse—' "

"That's enough hashtags," I said.

"Are you sure? I usually do a few more. I want to make sure it reaches more people, since it's a sponsored one," she said.

"You can always add more later if you want. Here's your phone," I said, handing it back to her. "I really have to go do some homework now."

It took everything within me not to add some extra hashtags, like #LoveYourBody or #AllBodiesAreGoodBodies. I walked such a fine line with her because, yes, she was my mom, but I also did not agree with her views on her body and my body, for that matter. How was I supposed to sit back and bite my tongue, like Ashley had suggested I do in her absence? How was I supposed to stand aside when she made me post things on her behalf that made me queasy? I just imagined all the girls my age, or the adults Mom's age, looking at her posts and feeling terrible about their bodies. I imagined them taking drastic measures like a juice cleanse to lose some weight in an unhealthy amount of time. And the fact that I played a small part in a post that could potentially make someone feel less confident about themselves and the body that they inhabited made me beyond upset.

But I bit my tongue. Because she's the mom, and I'm just the daughter.

chapter FIVE

The next week involved a lot of preparation of our home. It was a team effort between my mom and me to get the house *Shake the Weight*–filming ready. A big part of my role to get the house whipped into shape was purely keeping Fiyero entertained and out of all the new houseplants we'd bought. Apparently, they really touted the benefit of having plants in the home on the show, but Mom hadn't been able to keep a plant alive for more than a few weeks for my entire life. It was a wonder she raised two semifunctional children.

On the morning of, Mom and I sat in front of my closet, tilting our heads, trying to figure out the perfect outfit. The film crew had sent over a list of patterns and colors to avoid on camera, and in this moment, it seemed like those were the only clothes I owned. The subtle gene of the family totally went to Ashley. My philosophy was always the more color, the better.

"Do you have just a nice, plain blouse?" she asked. "Even a button-down?"

"Are we looking at the same closet right now?" I asked. I started scrounging through my drawers with my appropriately dubbed "boring clothes" until I found a denim button-down. "Can I at least wear red pants with this? I can't bring myself to do denim on denim. It's a fashion sin."

"Sure, whatever, they probably won't get much of your pants anyway," she said. "Come here; let's work on your hair."

I sat down on the edge of my bed while she worked her magic. She was always incredibly patient when it came to doing our hair or makeup, like it was a chance to step away from her stress and breathe for a second. Her fingers worked deftly on my hair, making the messy pile of blond curls into a French braid.

"Are you nervous?" I asked her.

She was silent for a few beats, threading my hair between her fingers. "Not as much as I thought I would be. I'm more scared for it to air than anything else."

"People loved you on that show," I said. "You have nothing to worry about."

She rested her hands on my shoulders, leaning around so that she could face me. She pecked a quick kiss on my cheek. "You mean that, baby?"

"I mean it," I said. "And I'm sorry about how I acted about the show earlier. I know how much it meant to you. Means to you."

"Thank you, sweet girl," she said. She rubbed her hands up and down my arms before declaring my French braid perfection. I looked down at my phone that blared with a fifteen-minute warning before the crew would be showing up. Mom rushed downstairs in a flurry, and I could hear her rearranging some last-minute things.

I decided that now would be a good time to send a quick text off to Ashley, to warn her that our family would be out of commission for the next few hours while the film crew was here.

Me: Getting ready to welcome the demons into our home.

Ashley: How's Mom?

Me: A little nervous. I'm trying to keep her calm.

Ashley: Try and keep it positive, k? For Mom's sake?

Me: I'm on my best behavior. Pinkie swear.

Ashley: Good. Love you. Proud of you. Call me when it's all done.

Me: Obvs. Love you, Sissy.

Ashley: Right back atcha. <3

The doorbell rang and Fiyero started to bark his head off from the next room. Apparently, he would be featured in a few clips in the video package, but for most of the shoot he would be banished to Ashley's room. If only we could trade places for the day. I'm sure America would love his little fluffy face more than having to look at mine during an interview.

I looked into the mirror on top of my vanity, which I'd had since my fifth birthday. All that I'd wanted that year was to have a princess bedroom, equipped with a canopy bed, a vanity, and a chandelier hanging from the ceiling. The canopy eventually became a safety hazard because I tangled myself in it as I slept, and the chandelier had been knocked down during an epic pillow fight from sleepovers past, but the vanity had stayed intact. It was this weird relic from my past that I somehow didn't hate. The perfect and intricate French braid and the makeup made me look like a stranger in my own mirror. This fake person I was about to become, the person who would smile and congratulate my mom for her success on a show that had done so much damage to her, was not something that I felt comfortable with.

"Savannah!" Mom yelled from the bottom of the stairs. That was my cue, whether I liked it or not. As I made my way downstairs, three men with camera equipment started bounding through the front door, setting up lighting in front of the couch in the living room. There was a woman wearing a headset with her cell in hand who was directing them to different parts of the house. A few other people flitted around our crowded entrance, waiting for instructions from the woman who was obviously in charge.

"Kim! It's wonderful to see you again, dear," the woman said, kissing both sides of Mom's face like she was an English socialite. You can't expect people to take your fanciness seriously when you're wearing Birkenstocks and shorts.

"Arden," Mom said back, pulling away. I knew it was taking everything in her not to wipe her cheeks off. Mom had a thing with germs. "Great to see you, too! Can I get you all anything?"

"Just your beautiful smile!" Arden said. She instructed a few of her minions still lingering around her to go wait in the living room with the cameramen. She finally took me in, and I could feel her eyes tracking up and down my person. I suddenly felt completely exposed, even though I was completely covered.

"This must be one of your lovely daughters," Arden said, smiling.

"This is my youngest, Savannah," she said, putting a hand on my back.

"I've heard so much about you and your sister," Arden said, collecting my fingers into a vise grip. "Now, my idea is to do the interviews first, then we'll get B-roll. Let's start with Kim. It will remind you of shoots during the show. Then we'll bring in Savannah."

She definitely picked up on the flinch and look of fear that came across me when she mentioned my being interviewed.

"Don't worry, dear, it won't take long. Ten minutes with you, max. I promise."

Even ten minutes sounded a little bit torturous. Regardless, I plastered on my best fake smile and hoped that it could last through this entire day.

I sat on the love seat kitty-corner from the couch, the official "on deck" position, as Arden called it. They had been interviewing Mom for the past ten minutes and were starting to get into the nitty-gritty of the questions.

"So, Kim, tell everyone how the show has changed your life at home," Arden prompted.

"I feel like I have my head on straight nowadays. I'm focused and determined to meet my goals each week and keep up with what *Shake the Weight* taught me. I keep inspirational messages sprinkled throughout the house for me and my girls to look at," she said.

"And how have your girls responded to your being on the show?" she asked.

My palms started to sweat waiting for her answer. The

smile that Mom had so perfectly been keeping up faltered for a moment before it shone even brighter.

"My girls have been incredibly supportive and have been making life changes alongside me. It's important to me that we are making changes that will keep everyone healthier for longer, and they seem to be taking to it really well," she said.

The lies spilled out of her mouth and sounded just like she'd probably rehearsed them so many times in front of the mirror. How was I supposed to follow up to that? Say that the thinspirations around the house were good for everyone? That her tiny backhanded comments about my weight inspired me to become fit? All both of those things did was make me feel worse and completely discourage me.

"Good, Kim. Can you say that quote again with a bigger smile at the beginning?" Arden asked.

Mom repeated the same sentiment, this time with more enthusiasm. It sounded true. It sounded like we were a family who rallied behind her extreme weight loss and wanted to follow suit. It was kind of a beautiful picture she painted, and for a moment, I wished it were true.

"Great. Okay, Savannah? It's your turn, dear," Arden said.

Mom came up from the couch and squeezed my shoulder as we traded spots. I wasn't sure if it was out of support or a warning to stick to the script. I suddenly felt like I might get sunburned under the harsh lights. I tugged at my denim button-down, wishing suddenly that I'd worn a color that didn't wash me out so horribly. That's what I get for grabbing something out of the boring clothes drawer.

"All right. Savannah, can you tell us about what it was like for your mom to get the call from *Shake the Weight* that we wanted her to be on the show? Do you remember that day?" Arden asked.

I could feel Mom's eyes boring into me. With the mixture of her gaze and the shining lights, my vision started to go fuzzy. My panic bubbled at the bottom of my stomach and started shooting itself through my veins, making me hyperaware of the amount of people staring at me. I took a deep breath through my nose and out of my mouth, in an effort to keep my anxiety at bay. It was hardly working.

"You need some water, dear?" Arden asked.

"I'll grab her a glass," one of the cameramen offered, sneaking away to the kitchen.

"I swear, I'll get you in and out as quick as possible, all right, sweetheart?" Arden asked.

I nodded my head, embarrassed that I was suddenly being pitied by this entire crew of strangers. The cameraman handed me a glass of water and I gladly took it, gulping about half of it before setting it down on the coffee table in front of me.

"Feeling good? Good. Let's start again," Arden said. "Tell

us about the day that you found out your mom was going to be on *Shake the Weight*."

"Uh, um, yeah. That day she got the call. It was . . . Mother's Day, I'm pretty sure. We were all eating dinner that Ashley had cooked when the phone rang. Mom dropped the phone when you guys told her who it was. After she was done talking to you guys, she went upstairs and started packing her bags for her screen test. We started packing our bags to stay with our dad for the weekend," I said.

Arden frowned at me, then motioned for the camera to quit rolling. The lights dimmed a bit, and I felt like I could breathe again.

"Can we make it a little bit more peppy, dear? We don't need the play-by-play. What were you all feeling in that moment? What was her excitement like?" Arden asked.

I nodded, and she motioned for them to start rolling again.

"She was really excited, so excited that she started packing her bags almost immediately after she got off the phone. It was nice to see her get excited about something again. It had been so long," I said.

"And why is that?" Arden pushed.

I looked to my mom. How personal was I supposed to get? Was I supposed to mention that my dad had an affair with her best friend? That their divorce had been a no-holding-back brawl?

"I mean, since the divorce and everything, she was not quite herself," I said.

Arden nodded. "What was it like watching her on TV?"

"It was really surreal. It was almost like she wasn't the same person when I saw her on TV. She acted completely different than she had my whole life. It was really weird to watch, actually. I wondered a lot about what she would be like when she came back. Whether she'd be my same mom."

"And is she?" Arden pressed.

"Yes and no," I said. "She's definitely happier. But she is not the same person who left last year."

Arden looked back at the cameramen and did the same motion that she had before. She came and sat next to me on the couch, resting her arm behind me, uncomfortably close.

"I feel like you mean that your mom is a better person thanks to the show, right? Do you want to try that clip again saying something more along those lines? We're trying to keep it positive here, dear, and you're bringing it down a little bit right now," Arden said.

"Sorry," I said, feeling my face burn. I couldn't look at Mom. This was her nightmare come to life—me not being able to say anything positive like she'd asked. The worst part about it all was I thought I was holding back.

"It's all right. Let's just try it again," she said, leaving her spot next to me on the couch. The lights turned back up to full brightness, and I squinted.

"My mom came back a completely different person after the show. And definitely for the better. I'm proud of all her hard work on the show," I said.

"That's more like it!" Arden said. "Now, Savannah, how has your life changed since your mom has been on the show?"

"People recognize us at the grocery store now," I said, which garnered a few giggles from everyone around us. "Other than that, my life hasn't changed too much."

"Has your mom inspired you to be healthier?"

"Inspired? *Forced* might be the better word. Wait, let me rephrase that. She makes conscious efforts to prepare healthy meals for my sister and me. It's a lifestyle change that we've had to adjust to . . . For the better!" I added hastily.

"Where's your sister today?" Arden asked.

"Oh, she's off being the dutiful college student. I wish I was there with her—learning and school gets me so excited. I'm sure she's having a blast learning from all the new people she's meeting. There's only so much you can do in a small town in Indiana where everyone knows all your business," I said.

"Okay, Savannah, I think that's all the questions I have for you. See? I promised. Quick and painless," Arden said.

I breathed the first sigh of relief I had all morning. As the cameramen set up a different angle for other shots, I sank into the couch next to Mom. I smiled her way, glad to finally be through with the hardest part of this process. She had her arms and legs crossed, and looked straight ahead, refusing to glance my way.

"Mom," I whispered.

"We're going to talk about this later, Savannah. I can't even look at you right now," she said.

Dread pooled in my gut. I thought I had done pretty well with the interview portion. I wasn't sure where this hostility from her was coming. Arden made sure that she got the good, positive clips that she needed.

After the crew left, Mom and a couple of her friends from work decided to go out for a celebratory drink. I was supposed to stay at home and watch Fiyero. Immediately after they left, I raced up to Ashley's room to let Fiyero out of his prison for the day. I nearly toppled over with the force he used to hug me when he saw me. I nestled my face into his fur while he tried to lick my face, one of my least favorite Fiyero tricks.

"I'm sorry you only got to come down for a few minutes, buddy," I said, scratching behind his ears. "I bet you were confused hearing our voices and not being able to come down and see us. I wish you could've been downstairs the whole time. I bet Arden wouldn't have had to cut off your interview."

He cocked his head like he was trying to understand me. I always believed that he was formulating his official response in dog language whenever he did that.

I pulled out my phone from my pocket and dialed Ashley, listening to the ringtone repeat again and again. It pushed me to her voice mail, and I frowned at my phone, hanging up. I texted her instead.

Me: Hey. Just tried to call you. Lots of dirt on the shoot today.

Ashley: I'm working on a group project. Call you tomorrow?

I sucked in a sharp breath, not realizing how close I had been on the verge of tears until I knew that Ashley wasn't available to talk me down. To remind me that everything would be okay and that I had tried my best with the interview. Pinprick tears started forming in the corners of my eyes, making my vision blurry.

Me: Okay. Talk to you tomorrow.

No "love yous" or "bye to you, toos" to be seen.

chapter SIX

The next morning, I woke up half expecting an apology text from Ashley for blowing me off yesterday. Instead, a text from an unknown number flashed on the front of my screen.

> **Unknown:** Hi Savannah. This is George. Grace gave me your number. I have a big test on Wednesday that I really need help studying for. Were you serious about being willing to tutor me?

My heart leaped. So he didn't hate me after the way we left things in the hallway. That, or he was really desperate for some help. Either way, I was ready to make it up to him for all my foot-in-mouth moments he'd been a witness to the past few weeks.

Me: Of course. How about this afternoon? One o'clock? My place?

George: My GPS remembers the way. See you then.

I had a lot of prep work to do if I was going to be entirely presentable for our tutoring session. Luckily, the house was still in decent shape thanks to the film crew's coming over yesterday. The reminder of the film crew made me cringe a little bit. Mom had been so angry with me, even though I tried to stay as positive as possible. I hadn't said anything completely awful, had I? She and her friends stayed out late getting drinks, and I decided to spend my wild Friday night doing research for the story Grace and I were working on.

With the help of Mrs. Brandt, I'd learned that all the school's funding was public record, and we filed to have the records sent to us. We found out they published an "overview" each year to the school's website, which generalized all athletics into one blanket number. We wanted to see the nitty-gritty.

The tenured salary for the school's baseball coach was just too high. Something fishy was definitely going on, and I was determined to get to the bottom of it.

I heard a small tapping at my bedroom door, and my stomach tightened. Mom opened my door and peeked her head in, and I closed my laptop, bringing my legs into a pretzel-style position.

"I think we need to talk about the show taping," she said, sitting down on the end of my bed. I wanted to pull my blankets up over my head and avoid this conversation at all costs, but it didn't seem like a very viable option at this point.

"Mom, I'm sorry about how it ended up going," I said. "But I do feel like they got some good footage to use where I was peppier."

"Do you know how reality TV works, Savannah? They want to sell the most dramatic story that they can. All that footage is going to be fair game for some editor who doesn't know us or care what the repercussions of our words will be. You've just handed them ammo," she said.

"Well, can't we ask Arden to look over it for us?"

Mom shook her head. "She can only control what she gets on camera. After that it goes over to the editing team. I just—I really hope that someone had a juicier story and they're going to focus more on that."

My stomach dropped to the floor. She rested her head in her hands as she sucked in a deep breath.

"What's done is done," she said.

"Mom—"

"I know you're sorry, Savannah. And I'll get over it, eventually. Right now I guess I'm just disappointed."

"How can I make it up to you?" I asked. I could stand Mom being angry at me, but the disappointment hurt me deep down. While anger rips through your body and tears at your guts, disappointment is a slow and painful ache that sits on your chest for much longer. I could deal with the rip and tear of her anger. Her disappointment was agony.

"I'll have to think on it," she said, getting up from the bed. I closed my eyes as I heard her footsteps pad back down the hallway and didn't open them again until I heard her bedroom door close.

———

Mom was playing catch-up on a client project for work, so she would be delightfully occupied while I prepared for my study session with George. I'd convinced her to keep Fiyero with her, on the off chance that George wasn't a dog person.

"George is Grace's cousin, right?" she asked.

I'd filled her in on some minor details about him, not daring to share the truth about my panic attack the day we met, or the harrowing moment when George almost turned me into a car pancake on the first day of school. I also definitely didn't tell her about the way my stomach fluttered thinking about him coming over, or the way I'd very vividly dreamed of us winning the three-legged race and him pulling me close after crossing the finish line.

"Yeah, that's him," I said, trying to play it cool. She saw right through it.

"Are you wearing eyeshadow?" she asked, smiling slightly.

"I study best when I feel my best, and rocking gunpowder smoky eye just really gets me in the mood for calculus," I said.

"I see," she said. "I'll keep Fiyero up here. Have fun with George."

Fiyero whined for a few moments as I closed the door to Mom's room. Once the door was firmly closed, I started on my quest to rid the house of anything marginally embarrassing for George to stumble upon.

It was officially 12:56 p.m. and I sat at our kitchen table, tapping my pencil anxiously. The mystery of not knowing if he was an early person (please, God, no), an on-time person (a little bit more acceptable), or a late person (much more my speed) was aggravating. This was why I very rarely hung out with new people—their unknown reactions made me more nervous than it was worth most of the time.

I meticulously tried to hide each motivational poster and throw pillow that Mom had scattered around the house in an effort to keep the words *weight loss* and *healthy lifestyle* out of the conversation in this house for the afternoon. I'd just finished shoving the EAT LESS SUGAR, YOU'RE SWEET ENOUGH ALREADY! pillow into the front closet when I heard a door slam in the driveway.

The clock had just switched to 12:57. An early person. I wanted to be more surprised by that fact than I actually was.

I swung the front door open to find him with his fist balled, ready to knock on my door. He took a step back, startled.

"I heard your car door and beat you to it," I said. "Come on in."

Having George in my house seemed strange, like two separate worlds of mine were colliding. As he took in the pictures of me and Ashley as kids displayed around my house, I suddenly wished that I'd picked a more neutral spot to meet. He was seeing a personal side to me that I normally didn't show the kids I tutored.

"Camp Snoopy?" he asked, pointing to a picture where I was sobbing while being forced to hold a mascot Snoopy's hand.

"That was back when the Mall of America was especially awesome. We went to Camp Snoopy every summer," I said.

"I think I have the exact same picture with my sister. Except she's the one screaming bloody murder," he said.

"I had a big distrust of mascot costumes. I'm still working on it, to be honest," I said.

I led him into the kitchen, where I'd set up our space with scrap paper, a handful of pencils, and a timer in case he wanted to take any practice quizzes. I personally work best under pressure, so the timer is always a good challenge to get the math juices flowing.

"So, what do you need the most help with?" I asked, pushing a piece of paper and a pencil in front of him. He took the pencil and started twirling it idly between his fingers.

He pulled out his textbook and plopped it in front of me, pointing to a section on quadratic functions.

"Quadratic functions? But they're four times the fun!" I said.

"Has anyone ever told you that you'd make the perfect Miss Frizzle in a *Magic School Bus* reboot?" he asked, smirking a tiny bit.

"Has anyone ever told you that Miss Frizzle is my hero and I take that as a compliment?"

"I've honestly never met someone so excited about math," he said. "Are you doing something with it in college?"

"I'm planning on going to Indiana State to study engineering," I said. "What about you? What are you planning to do after we break out of Springdale forever?"

"Probably something with music. I want go somewhere where there's a saxophone conservatory. I can't decide if I want to try to make it professionally or teach," he said.

"Ooh, anything to avoid having to teach little kids how to play. Ashley used to play flute back in the day, and that was rough to listen to in the house," I said.

He smiled. "That's actually my favorite part. I like helping kids realize that music is something they can work on their whole lives. Like it's a secret language they can speak with musicians around the world, no matter where they're from."

"That's actually really sweet," I said. We held eye contact for a few seconds before I looked back down at the textbook. "Okay. So, quadratic functions—"

"Can I have something to drink, before we get started?" he asked.

"Oh gosh, I'm officially the worst hostess ever. Yes. We have water, milk, orange juice, some diet pop—"

"Some diet what?" he asked.

"Pop," I said, emphasizing the final *p*. "You know, like Diet Coke."

"You mean soda," he said.

"I mean, you live in the Midwest now, George, you have to embrace *pop* over *soda* everywhere you go," I said.

"I'll have a diet, then," he said.

"A diet what?" I asked. "If you answer correctly I'll even pour it over ice for you."

"Pop," he cringed out, followed by a big smile. "Diet Coke is my weakness, otherwise I wouldn't have given in so easily."

"Sure," I said, putting on a smile that matched his. I brought the glass back to him, and he dramatically took a sip with a loud "Ahh!" at the end that made me giggle. I shuffled the paper in front of me, actually writing *Quadratic Functions, Chapter 3* on the top of the sheet before a very excited Fiyero bounded into the kitchen.

"Fiyero wanted to come say hi," Mom said, following closely behind him.

Fiyero practically pounced on George, trying his hardest to leave slobbery kisses on his face. George scratched Fiyero behind his ears, just like he loved, and they became instant best friends. It was easy to sway into Fiyero's favor—give him a table scrap or a particularly good scratch behind the ears and he was in the palm of your hand.

"George, you've now met poodle monster Fiyero. This is my mom," I said.

"Kim," she finished, shaking his hand.

"Nice to meet you, Kim." He smiled. I silently thanked

the gods that he didn't say Mrs. Alverson. That always put her in a weird funk when she had to explain that she was no longer, in fact, Mrs. Alverson.

"You're Grace's cousin, right?" Mom asked. I sent her a look, as if to warn her not to make it seem like we'd been talking too much about him. I wanted to seem like I at least had the smallest semblance of chill.

"I am," he said. "We moved here from South Carolina to be closer to family. Plus, my dad got a new job."

"That's a bummer that you had to switch schools your senior year," Mom said.

"Oh, I'm a junior, so it's a little less dramatic. Besides, I wasn't a huge fan of the school I went to in South Carolina. I think we all were in need of the change," he said.

A million questions popped into my brain. What happened at his old school? Why wasn't he sad to leave? Didn't he have friends he was leaving behind? It took everything in me to not start blurting them out as soon as I thought them.

"Well, I'm glad to hear you're having a better time here," Mom said. She looked between the two of us, and I widened my eyes in the universal teenage signal of "Leave us alone." She had a crooked smile on the corner of her mouth as she observed the signal.

"All right. I'll leave you two to it," she said. So we'd

formed some small form of peace since we talked this morning. Nothing had completely blown over, but at least we were talking again. I took it as a step in a positive direction.

She tried to convince Fiyero to go back upstairs with her, but he'd made a comfortable spot under the table, wrapped around George's foot. It didn't look like he'd be leaving anytime soon. Mom shook her head and went back upstairs, coffee in hand.

"He's not usually so comfortable with strangers," I said, pointing down to the sleepy mess of poodle fur at George's feet.

"I think he's probably comforted by our similar hairstyles," he said. "He must think I'm one of him."

I actually *snorted* with laughter and quickly covered my face in my hands. I would have never described George's strawberry blond curls as poodle-esque before, but now that he brought it up, the similarity was uncanny.

"Well, thankfully for you, it's a good look on both of you," I said.

He turned the same embarrassed shade of red all over that he'd turned in the hallway last week. I could feel my own face heating up from admitting that George might be a little, somewhat, kind of good-looking. You know, in a gangly seventeen-year-old boy kind of way.

"Thank you," he said. "I'll have to leave a nice review on the Yelp page for Supercuts, since you like it so much."

"Appreciated," I said.

"So Grace tells me that you're a really great writer," he said, twirling a pencil in his fingers.

"Have you been talking about me with Grace?" I asked, the smile that I was already wearing, spreading even farther across my face, if that was even possible.

"Only some basic recon. I had to make sure that you'd be a reputable tutor," he said.

"And my writing skills relate to that how?" I asked.

"I didn't ask Grace to give me that information. I also didn't ask for the information that you know all the words to every Eminem rap ever," he said.

"You're telling me you didn't also have a phase where you loved the 2002 classic movie *8 Mile*?" I asked.

"I don't think anyone our age did." He laughed.

"I am older than you, to be fair," I said.

"Barely!" he said.

"I'm old for my grade; I was born in September," I said.

"Well then, we're only eight months apart," he said.

"That's four and a half dog years."

"Just because I have poodle hair doesn't mean you can measure our ages in dog years," he said. "What's the one song . . . 'If you had one shot—' "

"Don't make me start, this could go all day," I said, giggling.

" 'Or one opportunity—' "

" 'To seize everything you ever wanted, in one moment, would you capture it, or just let it slip—' I'm going to stop, it's too much," I said, full-on belly laughing.

"I'm impressed," he said.

"Very few people get to witness Savannah Shady. You should feel honored," I said.

"Oh, I do," he said.

I shoved the paper that I'd written on so many minutes ago in front of him. "For *real* now. Quadratic functions . . ."

chapter SEVEN

In an effort to start making things up to my mom, I started my morning out by baking flaxseed pancakes from scratch. If I couldn't win at least a little bit of forgiveness from her favorite breakfast, this was going to be a long road back.

To pass the time, I tried to call Ashley, working off the chance that she happened to wake up before noon. Because I know if I were free to sleep as long as I wanted, there is a 1,000,000 percent chance I would wake up at dinnertime every day.

"Sissy?" she asked.

"Sissy! You're awake!" I said.

"I am now," she grumbled.

"Sorry," I said, genuinely sorry that my suspicion was correct. "Mom and I finally had a big fight about the show."

"Are you okay?" she asked.

"I think I will be," I said. "She did that whole 'I don't know how you can make it up to me,' and 'I'm not mad, I'm just disappointed' thing. Which is worse than her flat-out yelling."

"Aw, babe," she said.

"I wish you could come home," I said, taking a bite out of the fresh pancakes. "I'm not sure that I can handle our episode of *Shake the Weight* airing without you."

"Maybe you'll make up before then," Ashley said.

"Highly unlikely. Mom has a strict one-week return on firm grudges. At least. Trust me, I should know, being the one who inspires most Mom grudges," I said.

"Maybe she'll make an exception, since you're living alone together. I'm going to be optimistic about this one," she said.

"Thank goodness for your optimism. I almost believe that she'll come down in a chipper mood this morning like nothing has happened," I said.

"Can I call you back later?" she asked abruptly. "I stayed up way too late last night."

"Sure! Yeah, sorry I woke you," I said.

"S'fine," she mumbled. "Talk later."

"Love you!" I said, as she hung up the phone.

A few minutes later, I heard Mom's door creak open

slowly. She made her way down the stairs, then shuffled into the kitchen as I put on my biggest possible smile.

"Mom, I made some flaxseed pancakes for you. What do you want on them?" I asked.

"I'm not hungry," she mumbled.

"Are you sure? I made these all healthy for you," I said.

She ran her hands through her bed-head hair and sighed. "I actually might just go back to bed," she said.

"At least take this up with you," I said, handing her the plate of pancakes. "It would be silly to let them go to waste."

"Fine," she said.

So apparently the peace she feigned when George was over was fake. Noted.

———

When I thought I was more alone than ever after the first day Ashley was at school, I had no idea how lonely it would be with Mom checked out, too. She sulked in her room for as long as she possibly could before going to work every day. Every time I tried to engage her, she would come up with an excuse to leave the room.

I invited Grace over the night that our episode of *Shake the Weight* was going to be airing as moral support, since Mom had been MIA the entire week. She brought over some calc homework for us to work on before it started, along with her favorite tropical pack of jelly beans. I never understood her obsession with jelly beans, but she swore that they got her in the mind-set to study.

"How are you feeling about making your television debut?" she asked, popping a jelly bean into her mouth.

"Appropriately nervous," I said. "I have pre-embarrassment."

"Come on, it won't be that bad," she said.

"I hope you're right," I said. I started to work on another page of homework, scribbling my way through the worksheet.

"So how did studying with my cuz go?" she asked.

"Oh, last week? With George? That was good. Great? We're no longer in a world-war situation if that's what you're asking. I wouldn't say that we're *friends*, but, you know. Civil," I said.

She stared at me for a few beats before a sneaky smile crept onto her face. "You totally have a crush on my cousin."

"I wouldn't say that," I said.

"First Mateo, now George . . . I don't think you should be allowed around any more of my family members," she teased.

"We had a nice time. That's it. He didn't even text me to tell me how he ended up doing on the test, so I don't think it's going to happen again or anything," I said. Besides, there was no way he was interested in me.

"Well, did you ask him to text you with his results?" she asked.

"No," I said, grabbing a handful of her jelly beans.

"He's not a mind reader, Savvy. If you want people to text you again, tell them that you want them to text you," she said.

We heard the stairs creak behind us as Mom emerged from her bedroom for the first time since she got home from work. She plastered a smile on her face when she saw Grace.

"What a nice surprise to see you here, Grace," she said.

"I couldn't miss Savvy's TV debut," Grace said, sending a matching smile back to her.

"It's on in two minutes," Mom said, sinking into the couch. She pulled out her phone, no doubt getting ready to live tweet the episode. I turned up the volume on the TV and waited for the heavy beating of the drums from the *Shake the Weight* theme song to take over the living room.

Lauren McVey, the hostess of *Shake the Weight*, graced our TV screen once again, and I sucked in a scared breath. We had no idea where our package would fit in with the rest of the contestants from Mom's season, and we had no idea how much I would be featured. Maybe it was a good thing that Grace was here. Mom would at least try to keep it together a little bit better for Grace's sake.

"Do you want any jelly beans, Kim?" Grace asked.

"Oh, gosh no, honey. Savannah, if you want a snack, there are banana chips in the kitchen," she said. And there it was, even minutes before she was going to possibly have a breakdown from seeing her daughter make a mockery of her on national television, she could still get a jab in about what I should be eating. It made the jelly beans that I'd already swallowed turn in my stomach.

After two of the other contestants from Mom's season flashed across the screen, next was Mom's face. She was out in the backyard running around with Fiyero, laughing as he raced around her. I turned around to look at Mom's face, which was sunken in, like she was holding her breath during the entire segment.

Mom talked about how much the show had changed her, and how it gave her the confidence to truly be herself, all with photos from her childhood montaged on top of her voiceover. Just when I thought my heart couldn't take any more, Lauren McVey's voice played over a shot of me looking unamused in between interview takes.

"But not everyone on your journey is always going to be a positive supporter," Lauren McVey said. My blood ran completely cold and I could not move for the next minute of television that unfolded in front of us.

"My mom came back a completely different person after the show," I said, as they played footage of me looking bored or mad during the interview. It then switched to B-roll of me sitting at the kitchen table, twirling a fork while Mom laughed at Fiyero from across the room. A moment when I thought they hadn't been rolling.

Lauren McVey's voice came over like she was the interviewer that day and not Arden the producer. "For the better, though, right? Hasn't she inspired you?"

"Inspired? *Forced* might be the better word. It's a lifestyle change that we've had to adjust to. People recognize us at the grocery store now. There's only so much you can do in a small town in Indiana where everyone knows all your business."

Lauren took over the screen and was shaking her head. "This is a small reminder that not everyone is going to be completely supportive of your journey. But it's up to you to keep pushing through and do what's right for you. After the break, we'll catch up with Anna Marie and her family in Austin, Texas."

The sound of the commercial for stain-resistant pants took up the entire space of our living room. I didn't dare look at any of them, knowing that if I did, I would absolutely burst into tears. The editors had made a hack job of my interview, picking and choosing parts of my quotes to include to make me look as evil as possible. Like the heartless, fat daughter who is taking out her jealousy of her mom's new life in her interview. Every part of it made me sick.

Grace's hand clasped over mine and she squeezed. I couldn't squeeze back, completely frozen in my place. Arden had promised that she would make everything positive. She even had me reshoot answers to have a more positive spin! Maybe that was what they were doing all along—trying to get me to say the most ridiculous things possible while reassuring my mom that they were trying their best to make me look good. I knew better the entire time leading up to the filming. I knew how toxic and manipulative reality TV could be, let alone a show that ridicules people about their weight on a national scale. Even so, I was dumbfounded.

Finally, after a few moments, I had the courage to look back at Mom. She was still staring at the screen, unable to fully process the train wreck that was her segment. Her eyebrows furrowed together as she stood up, becoming a towering giant over me.

"I warned you about the interview," she said coolly. Too coolly. With ice dripping in every word. "But, of course, you did whatever you wanted to do instead. I can't even speak to you right now. I can't—" she said.

"Mom," I started, the giant lump of holding back tears forming in my throat.

"You knew how much this meant to me," she said. "You *promised*."

"I'm sorry—"

"Grace, I'm sorry that you had to see this," she declared, looking around. She snatched her keys from the hook by the front door.

"Don't drive when you're upset," I said, my voice reaching new octaves while trying to hold back tears.

"Newsflash. I'm the mom. You're the kid. I will do exactly what I want, when I want," she said. She slammed the front door behind her without looking back. I heard Norma the Nissan starting up since Grace had boxed Mom's car in the driveway. Grace and I sat in silence as the headlights from Norma continued down the road.

Once they were out of sight, I completely burst into full-on, ugly sobs.

"This is not about you," Grace said, tracing circles on my back.

"I said those things, Grace," I managed. "They edited it, but I said them."

"Because you meant them!" she said. "Screw them for making you talk about something that you don't agree with. Screw them for twisting the words that actually came out of your mouth."

"I just wanted to be supportive," I said. Because I did. I wanted to be the calm, collected sister Ashley told me I could be. I wanted to be the strong peacemaker while she was out of the house. I wanted to have a normal relationship with my mom again without her obsession with weight getting in the way of everything.

"I think you've been pretty damned supportive," Grace said. "I know your sister will never say this because she would never say anything bad about your mom, but she's being incredibly unfair to you. Making those backhanded comments to you about everything you eat? That is the definition of uncool parenting behavior."

"Because we both know so much about parenting," I said.

"I know that parents shouldn't be allowed to make their kids feel like shit unless they buy into their culty dogma," she said.

I shrugged. "I don't think she does any of it on purpose."

"Does that matter?" Grace asked. "She's not looking out for you when she makes those comments. She's looking out for her own self-interest."

"She's the mom. I'm the kid," I said, repeating Mom's rant. "I just have to deal for now until I can leave this place."

"What about living with your dad for a while?" Grace asked.

I snorted. "With Sheri? Two months of living with them was almost enough to drive me over the edge."

"I'm just saying, you have other options. You don't have to stay here," Grace said.

"I appreciate it, but we're fine. It's fine here. I can make it until college," I said.

She held out her arms so that I could fall into a hug. "I've always got your back, babe. It's us against the world."

Grace offered to stay with me until Mom got back, but it was reaching dangerously close to her curfew, and I convinced her that I would be okay if she left. Every part of me wanted to ask her to stay, to ask her if I could hang out at her house for the foreseeable future, but I couldn't bring myself to be that kind of burden.

I lay down in my bed, my legs curled into my chest. I'd read online that creating pressure around your torso was supposed to be comforting when you were having a panic attack, but it just made me feel like I was suffocating. I changed my position so that I was starfished across the bed and felt the tremors shake out to the tips of my fingers and toes. My breathing slowly changed from ragged and quick to a more even rhythm as the panic left my body.

Why hadn't Ashley called me yet? If she'd seen the show, she had to know that I would be freaking out right now. One part of my brain tried to remind me that she was probably studying or hanging out with friends and hadn't had the chance to watch the show yet. The other part of my brain tried to convince me that she was mad at me, too. That she's warned me about keeping the peace while she was gone, and she was angry that I'd so publicly disrupted it.

My fingers started dialing a number that I'd known by heart since I was a little girl without me even realizing it.

"Savannah?" my dad asked as he answered the other end of the line. I held my breath for a few moments, realizing just what a mistake I might have made in calling him. Maybe if he couldn't hear my breathing, he'd hang up.

"Savannah, I know you're there," he said.

"Hi," I squeaked out.

"It's late. What's wrong?" he asked.

"Did you watch the show?" I asked.

"We have a strict no–*Shake the Weight*–viewing policy now," he said.

I twisted my blanket in my fingers idly and tried to remember the last time we talked on the phone. It had to be months ago.

"It was really bad, Dad. They came and interviewed me for a follow-up, and I looked like such a brat. Mom is so mad at me," I said.

He sighed. "She knew how you felt about that show. She knew how we all felt about it. She should have known going into this interview that it wouldn't be full of glowing praise."

"I tried so hard to make her happy, Dad. I—I don't know if she'll ever forgive me for this," I said.

"She'll forgive you. Just give it time," he said.

"Could I wait it out with you for a while?" I asked. He was silent for a few beats.

"You're in the middle of school. You can't just drive an hour to school and back each day," he said.

"Could I come for a week then? Just to give her some time to cool off?" I asked. The last sentence came out with a crack of tears. I'd never asked him something like this. I'd always been so firmly on Team Mom through their entire divorce that I'd never even considered moving to Walcott with him of my own free will. This was his chance to do something nice for me.

"Now's not the best time, Savannah," he said. "Sheri is remodeling our house, and I just don't think this is a good time to have guests."

"I'm not a guest. I'm your kid," I said. My sadness was turning quickly to anger. The little piece of hope that I'd built around this idea of getting a relationship back with my dad was slowly crumbling inside a little place in my heart I'd ignored for a while now.

"I'm sorry, you just can't come—" he said.

I hung up the phone before he could finish his sentence.

———

The next day at school I got a few weird looks in the hallway from the handful of kids who would tune in to *Shake the Weight* on Wednesday nights. Where the kids who recognized me or my mom used to smile at me as they passed, they quickly dropped eye contact and walked away today. They realized that they didn't want to mess with the new "Reality TV Brat," as I was dubbed by a particularly snarky blog. Trust me, I'd seen it all in the recaps this morning. It was a good thing that I'd already set all my accounts to private the moment that Mom went on the show, otherwise I was sure there would be a flood of hate mail for me all over social media.

The warning bell rang, letting me know that first-period calc was ten minutes away. I started to head toward Mr. Kavach's room, looking everywhere for Grace. If there was one day I needed her as my wingwoman, it was today. So, of course, she was nowhere in sight.

"Savannah?" I heard from behind me.

I turned around to take in George, having to completely tip my head back to make eye contact with him. For some reason, I hadn't noticed how ridiculous our height difference was until that moment. We had to have a good foot in between our heights. The ends of his strawberry blond curls were still a little damp, like he'd just woken up late and had to take a supersonic shower before driving to school.

"How are you?" he asked.

"Oh," I said, turning away from him and continuing my walk toward Kavach's room. "Did you watch the show? It's okay if you don't want to associate yourself with me anymore. The rest of the Internet has already written me off."

"What?" he asked. "Wait, what show? Are you holding out on your fame on me over here?"

I turned back to him. "Grace didn't tell you? You really don't know?"

"I truly don't know what you're talking about," he said.

"My mom, she was on that show *Shake the Weight* last season. They came back a few weeks ago for a follow-up interview with the families, and it aired last night. My interview did not put me in the best light, to say the least," I said.

"Then my question still stands," he said. "How are you?"

The sincerity of it sent a shiver up my spine. His sincerity floored me. There was nothing sarcastic in that moment, no more banter left in him.

"I'm doing okay, thank you," I said, deepening our eye contact.

"Good," he said, before turning that full-body shade of

red and turning his eyes from my gaze. "Uh, I do have a question for you."

"Ask away," I said, starting up my walk to class again.

"So we have a precalc test on Friday that I need some help with. I can pay you in a milkshake and endless fries if you're game?" he asked.

"Call it pizza and you have a deal," I said. "Want to meet at the Pizza Kitchen tonight? Five o'clock?"

"That's the other thing," he said. "My mom needs the car tonight. Do you mind picking me up?"

"I can't promise that we'll get there in one piece, but I can give you a ride," I said. "Driving is one of my least favorite pastimes."

The one-minute warning bell struck and he froze, probably not realizing just how little time he had to make it to his first class.

"I have to get going," he said.

"Wait!" I called after him, "I don't have your address!"

"I'll slip a note in your locker!" he yelled back, as he ran down the hallway.

"How do you know which one is mine?" I asked.

"I just do!" he yelled back over his shoulder, sending me a lopsided smile before he rounded the corner.

chapter EIGHT

S ure enough, when I went to my locker before leaving for the day, a piece of notebook paper folded into a triangle fluttered to the floor. When I opened it up, it had his address underlined at the top with monument-centric directions (my favorite kind of directions) listed below.

111 S. Berlin St.

Take a right off your street

Head toward the Circle K with 80 oz. slushies

Turn left at the corner of CK and that yellow house with antique ducks in the front lawn

Turn left at the fire hydrant that Grace hit with her car last year

If you reach the woman telling fortunes at the end of Berlin, you've gone too far.

———

I completed the typical routine of letting Fiyero out and playing with him in the backyard for a half hour after getting home for the day. I set an alarm on my phone to remind me to get presentable by four thirty. Properly de-sweating before my studying with George involved a variety of deodorants, spritzers, and baby powder for my hair. I turned on two small fans in my bathroom to get the ball rolling, airing out all the sweat that had accumulated after my playtime with Fiyero. Fiyero hated fans, so he sat in the hallway, completely avoiding my flurry of preparation.

I left a note for Mom on the counter to tell her where I was. Not that I thought that she particularly cared at the moment. We still hadn't spoken since the episode aired last night, and no matter how hard Ashley tried to get us to reconcile from afar, she wouldn't budge. I think last night possibly invoked one of the largest Mom Grudges to have ever taken hold in our house. It would probably take weeks for me to thaw out the frozen wall she'd built between us.

I put a very distraught Fiyero back in his kennel and promised that Mom would come home to let him out soon.

Norma the Nissan and I made our way down my street and turned right, just like George's creative directions had said. Even though I'd figured out which house was probably his in my head, I still made sure to hit all the landmarks that he talked about in his note, laughing especially hard as I came across that fateful fire hydrant that Grace broke her car's grill on.

George was sitting on his front porch when I pulled up, and he stood when he saw my car come into view. I was extra careful to keep Norma as far away as possible from his mailbox and any of his neighbors' cars. He'd made a complete outfit transformation, ditching his band T-shirt and jeans for a button-down and khakis. The sleeves on his button-down were just the tiniest bit short, like he'd hit a growth spurt overnight. He tugged at them before he opened the passenger-side door.

"If I knew we were being classy Pizza Kitchen patrons, I would have dressed up more," I said as he sat down.

His face turned its embarrassed shade of red, but he laughed it off like a champ. "I dress to impress. You never know who you might see at the Pizza Kitchen."

"Expecting anyone in particular?" I asked.

"No," he said quickly. "But you can never be overdressed. There's an official clichéd saying about it and everything."

"I think there might be a line of being overdressed for

the Pizza Kitchen that you are on the border of crossing," I said.

He looked down at his phone for a second before looking back at me. "Do you think I should change then?"

"What? No," I said. "You look nice. I'm giving you a hard time, Smith."

He nodded, wiping his hands on his pants. I knew that I wasn't the most reliable driver in the world, but I didn't know what was making him so antsy. He kept bouncing his legs up and down and fidgeted with the radio the entire way to the Pizza Kitchen.

When we pulled up, the parking spots were very limited. I managed to squeeze in next to a giant SUV that boxed me in to my side. George got out fine on his end and closed the door. I opened my door about an inch and realized that there was no level of sucking in my stomach that could help me get out that way. With no other choice, I climbed over the middle console of the car, banging my knee on the way across. When I went to open the handle, the door opened on its own and George held out a hand.

"You could have reparked," George said as I took his hand.

"We would have been sitting here for another ten minutes if I tried to adjust. Trust me, I just saved you a lot of frustration," I said.

He kept my hand in his for a few extra moments and I swear he could feel how hard my heart was beating in the palm of my hands. Somehow, it didn't seem to faze him. He continued on into the Pizza Kitchen while I rubbed my hand where we'd just been touching.

We were seated at a table in the back of the restaurant, the perfect vantage point to spy on the town of Springdale as they fled into one of the only pizza places in town for a Thursday-night meal. Some of my neighbors walked in and waved at me before sending a confused look about the mystery boy sitting across from me at the table. I felt like I needed a neon sign that said "I'm tutoring him. He doesn't like me like that."

He pulled out his textbook and flipped to chapter four, spinning it so I could take a look. He'd underlined the word *Rational* in the chapter title and written a small *ha* next to it. I was taking it that rational functions were not seeming as rational to him as the name might suggest. I peeked at one of the practice problems in the book and solved it on some scratch paper, checking my answer in the back of the book.

"How did you do that so quick?" he asked.

"My brain just likes solving problems," I said. "I don't know why."

"I'm very jealous," he said.

"Well, I'm jealous that your brain helps you read music.

I tried to play the violin in fourth grade and could never get the hang of the whole 'looking at sheet music and having to play an instrument without looking at the same time' thing," I said.

"That's different—you could have learned how to read music quicker if you stuck with it for longer," he said.

"And you can learn to solve math problems quickly if you practice at it," I said.

"What kind of pizza are you feeling tonight?" he asked. "My treat, especially if you're trying to rewire my brain to be a math brain. We might be here all night."

"I'm always down for a classic flavor. Pepperoni? Sausage? All good with me," I said.

"I've heard rumors that they have a delicious Hawaiian pizza," George said.

I groaned. Of course, he's related to Grace. Their entire family is addicted to pineapple on pizza.

"Pineapple and pizza are two p's that should never mix. I'm a pizza purist," I said.

"We can't be friends now," he said, crossing his arms, even with a smirk on his face.

The waiter walked up right in that moment, looking between George and me. "What can I get you?" he asked.

"Half pepperoni, half pineapple," I said.

George raised his eyebrows. "You sure?"

"Don't make me second-guess myself," I said. What can I say? He made me want to compromise. We both ordered a round of Diet Cokes before I pointed back down at his homework.

"As boring as it sounds, I learn the most from taking a practice quiz, seeing where I still need to practice, and then taking another practice quiz at the end of my study session to see if I improved. Do you want to try that? Maybe we'll be a little more productive this way," I said.

He groaned. "I'll try it. But I'm a pretty awful test taker."

"This is seriously no pressure. I'm an official judgment-free zone, and this practice quiz will in no way affect your grade," I said. I watched as his previously tensed shoulders started to relax a bit. "You know, Mr. Kavach is pretty judgment-free, too. If that helps when you're taking tests."

"I wish you could just sit in there with me while I'm taking a quiz and be my math Yoda. It's the atmosphere of it all—it's so quiet, all you can hear are pencils scraping against paper, and every part of me wants to look over at the people's tests around me to see where they are. But then, when I get a glimpse and see that I'm behind, it sends me into this new anxious spiral that I can't pull myself out of. It's—it's kind of debilitating sometimes," he said.

He was wringing his hands the entire time he explained his test anxiety and I wanted to reach out and grab them. I wanted to reassure him that he would be okay, and that he wasn't the only person in the world who felt this way.

"Have you ever asked Kavach if you could come in early in the mornings before school and take your quizzes and tests? I bet he would be pretty accommodating," I said.

"I don't need special treatment. I'll just deal with it," he said, retreating within himself.

"Wouldn't it be worth it if it helped you show your true ability?" I asked.

He considered it for a moment. "I'll think about it."

"Good," I said. I pulled out the practice quiz that I'd scrounged up from my precalc workbook from last year and set it on the table in between us. "Do you feel like you want to take this now? If not, we can totally work on something else."

"I'll take it," he said, pulling the papers in front of him. He stared down at them for a few seconds, and then his eyes slid back to mine.

"I promise I won't be watching you! I have stuff to read for the story Grace and I are working on."

He cracked each of his knuckles and twirled the pencil around in his fingers for a few moments before he started working. I watched him briefly before keeping my promise and pulling out my laptop.

The public records that I'd requested for the history of

the athletic department's salaries had come in, and they'd been sitting hot in my in-box until I had a chance to look at them. It was the first time that this story really felt *real* and like it could potentially have a big impact on my community. The exhilaration from that realization made me a little giddy, if I was being honest with myself.

First, I pulled up the information for the head baseball coach, Coach Triad, since he seemed to be the sketchiest of the bunch. For the most part, his salary made a gradual upturn year over year (considering he was one of the oldest teachers at Springdale High School) until the year 2000. That year, there was a $10,000 bonus attached to his salary, and that was then added to his base salary moving forward.

I quickly went to the *Spartan Spotlight*'s archives online, which someone had thankfully converted to online files in the last few years. I scrolled through 2000's newspapers, looking for something that would indicate a spike.

All I could find in the sports section was that there was a whole slew of kids who were going to play for Indiana Tech on scholarship. No one stood out; there was no scandal that would have pushed him to ask for a pay raise to stay—nothing.

I was about to comb through the opinions sections from

the 2000s for any insight into what the school's climate might have been like during that time, but George had finished his quiz in tandem with our pizza showing up.

"I vote we both take a break and enjoy this blasphemous pizza together," I said.

"Deal," he said, already grabbing a slice.

The pepperoni tasted glorious, and I couldn't even tell that it had been cross-contaminated by pineapple. I don't think either of us realized how hungry we were until we both dug in.

"Do you have any fun plans for the weekend?" he asked, popping a single pineapple piece into his mouth.

"Ashley's finally coming home," I said. "It's been three weeks. I'm excited for the house to feel back to normal again."

"I'm glad I'm the oldest," he said. "I don't know if I could handle my parents' undivided attention. I guess my sister, Hannah, will have to deal with that when the time comes."

"Hannah can join my left-behind-siblings support group. Thankfully, she has another year to prepare herself," I said. "How about you? Anything exciting going on?"

"We have some extra practice for a jazz band competition coming up. We've got a *lot* of work to do," he said.

A single pepperoni slid off the top of my pizza and fell

onto my lap, leaving a greasy stain on my new white dress. I was playing pizza roulette by opting to keep my napkin on the table rather than in my lap, so I should have known better.

"I'm officially oh for one with stains. How are you fairing?" I asked.

"I'm golden." He smiled. "Just more proof that pineapple is the superior topping."

"Yeah, yeah," I said, smirking.

I could eat pizza and chat with George for forever and a day and never get tired of it.

Finally, Saturday rolled around and I got text confirmation that Ashley was ten minutes away from our house. She was hitching a ride with one of her classmates that she was on-again, off-again friends with, and she was live-texting me the entire conversation they were having about Indiana State's frat party scene. AKA, Ashley wanted to jump out of the car fifteen minutes into the conversation.

> **Ashley:** If she tells me one more time about how her boyfriend is reigning boom cup champion I swear . . .
> **Me:** Tuck and roll out the door when you see the house, just tuck and roll.

I passed the next few minutes very impatiently from the comfort of my room, scrolling absentmindedly through Twitter without really taking anything in. The occasional cute puppy GIF might hold my attention, but it was a very rare occurrence. The power of the puppy GIF is strong.

"Family!" I heard yelled from a singsongy voice downstairs that only belonged to one person. I raced down the stairs, opening my arms to her immediately.

A hug from my big sister was arguably one of the best in the world. She made me feel safe and important all at once, in the most genuine way that anyone in the world could. I sighed with relief.

"It's so great to see you," I said. "We have so much to catch up on! I want to know all about your friends at school. How's that one girl, Yael? Are you two a thing yet? Still working on it?"

"Definitely not a thing yet," she started. "But I've made the best friends. They drag me out on adventures every weekend so that I don't stay cooped up in my dorm. I think I've found my group, you know? I never really had a group of people I could depend on in high school, but now I think I've found them."

"That makes me super happy," I said. "You deserve to have a group."

"Thanks, Sissy," she said, wrapping her arm around my neck. "Where's Mom?"

"She's out on a run with Fiyero," I said. At the mention of Fiyero, Ashley's eyes widened. Like she had almost forgot how glorious her reunion with the poodle monster would be.

"How's my puppy baby doing?" she asked.

"As cuddly as ever," I said. "Don't worry, though, he still sleeps on your bed even when you're not here."

"Aw! That is the sweetest and saddest thing I've ever heard!" she said.

The front door jiggled, and we both snapped our heads in that direction. The blur of white fur was the first thing that flew through the front door, and Ashley squealed in a very un-Ashley-like manner. Fiyero promptly tackled Ashley to the ground and covered her face in a million slobbery kisses. It was truly the reunion of a century.

"My baby's home!" Mom said, rushing over to Ashley and Fiyero. Once he had his fair share of kisses, Mom pulled Ashley up from the ground and planted ten of her own kisses on Ashley's head.

"I missed you, Mama," Ashley said, wrapping her in a full hug. "So much that I don't care that you're sweating all over me."

They both giggled as Mom instructed her to twirl

around, to make sure that she didn't miss anything that had changed about her over the three weeks since we saw her. Mom held a hand up to the top of Ashley's head and compared it to her height.

"Have you been growing? Things were not supposed to change so much in just three weeks," she said.

"I'm growing, but I don't think by height," Ashley said.

"Of course you are, sweet girl," Mom said, pulling her into another hug. "Savvy, will you help Ashley carry her laundry upstairs? Holy smokes, kid, have you not done any since you left?"

"I can't do it like you do," she said.

"Yeah, yeah," she said. "You're lucky I missed you!"

Ashley and I each tugged a bag of laundry up the stairs, trying our best to keep it from dragging us back downstairs in the opposite direction. From the weight of my bag, you would have believed that there was a body inside.

"How does one produce so much dirty laundry?" I asked.

She huffed out a tired laugh. "I wear multiple outfits in a day, Sav! There's a comfortable outfit that you wear to class, a going-out outfit for the later part of the day, and then cute pajamas because your whole dorm floor will see you in them on the walk from your room to the bathroom. It's a very high-stakes fashion competition at all times."

"That sounds stressful," I said.

We dumped the bags in front of the washer and dryer before she led me into her room. She ceremoniously jumped face-first onto the pink tie-dyed comforter she'd picked out when she was twelve and let out a big sigh.

"Savor your favorite places in this house while you still can, Savvy," she said. "Coming back home after moving out feels . . . disorienting. Almost like these spots were never really mine in the first place."

"Don't say that! This is your bed, the bed that you've slept in for the last six years of your life, in the room that you've stayed in for the last twelve years of your life. You've been away for three weeks!" I said.

She sighed again, wrapping the comforter around her. "But it feels so final, you know? Like, I'll never move back in here as the kid who would pick out this god-awful comforter. When I come back here from now on, I'll be a guest."

I joined her on the bed, and she opened up one side of the comforter to wrap me in with her. We were a sister burrito. We stayed this way for a few minutes, neither one of us feeling like we had anything else to add. I just wanted to bask in this moment, this feeling of being whole again in a house that had made me feel so empty for the last few weeks.

chapter NINE

I have to say, when my fantasies took place in the boys' locker room, I did not envision holding an interview with the seventy-year-old baseball coach first thing on a Monday. We sat in the middle of the ungodly smelly room with a tiny recorder in between us and a notebook in my hand. He looked less than enthusiastic to be speaking with me, but part of Springdale High's new "transparency initiative" involved leaders needing to be more available for press interviews. And, in this case, I'm press.

Mrs. Brandt had prepped me, warning me that Coach Triad would be less than forthcoming and would probably have some prepared answers that he'd consulted on with the school's PR team. But she'd helped me come up with a few questions to catch him off guard and make him a bit more candid.

"So, Mr. T. Can I call you Mr. T?"

"No," he said, adjusting his hat.

"Cool. Mr. Triad. Can you tell me—"

"Coach T," he said.

"Excuse me?" I asked.

"You can call me Coach T," he said.

"Very specific. Noted," I said. "Coach T, can you tell me about your experience being the baseball coach at Springdale? How many years have you been here?"

"I've been here for over forty years. Coaching this team has been one of the best experiences of my life. I was a Spartan back in the day, and being able to pass down that legacy for years to come means everything to me," he said.

"That's sweet," I said. I wrote down *baseball is an incestuous lovefest* in my notes. "And how many years have you been working alongside Jolene Foster?"

"Who?" he asked.

"Jolene Foster, the dance team coach," I said.

"That's her name now? They come and go so quick that I can never learn all their names. She's blond, right? Cute dimples?"

I wrote down *pervy old man* in my notes. "Yes, she's blond. So why do you think they have such a high turnover rate?"

"I don't know, their husbands get new jobs? They start having kids? It beats me," he said.

FUCK THIS OLD DUDE, I wrote in my notes.

"Do you think it has anything to do with their salaries?" I asked.

"I'm sure they get paid a fine amount for what they do," he said.

"Well, according to public record, you make a tenured salary of sixty-five thousand dollars a year and growing each five years that you stay, while Ms. Foster's salary is under twenty thousand dollars a year. The salary for this position has not changed in over ten years, even though our dance team has won state competitions the last two years in a row. Do you feel like that's fair pay for what she does?" I asked.

"How did you figure out my salary?" he asked.

"It's public record. Could you please answer my question? Do you think it's fair pay for what she does?" I asked.

"Well, I suppose not," he said.

"The dance team practices every afternoon after school in the gym and has for years. They are preparing for their state competition in two months. It was brought to my attention that the baseball team recently took over their spot without warning and outside of their typical training season. Is this correct?"

"I didn't know that they use that space," he said.

"Really? In your over forty years here, you didn't know that the dance team uses the gym in the afternoons during the first quarter of school?" I asked.

He squirmed in his seat. "Well, I guess I had an idea. But our team is bigger than ever this year. We needed a larger spot to start our HIT—high-intensity training—for the season. The gym is the natural spot."

"So you overtook the dance team's space outside of your competition season because you felt entitled to it?" I asked.

He scrunched up his face before standing from the wooden benches that we squatted on in the locker room. "I don't enjoy your tone. I've answered enough of your questions."

"That's fine with me. Do you have anything else you'd like to add, on the record? Any remorse for taking over their spot?" I asked.

"I don't have any remorse. They keep me around for a reason. They pay me more for a reason," he said.

"And what reason is that?" I asked.

"You don't see the dance team bringing in revenue for the school. You don't see them bringing in recruiters. It's just the way the world works, doll. I'm sorry to say," he said.

He hobbled his way out the door, and I sat back down, looking over all my notes. I had some gold here. Now all I had to do was investigate the revenue that the baseball team was *actually* bringing in for the school, if recruiters were doing any shady gift giving to the school/coach behind closed doors, and seriously get an interview with Jolene Foster. If she had to put up with this crotchety old man for any longer than five minutes, I felt horrible for her.

The first person I wanted to tell about the interview was Grace. She'd be so excited to hear all the juicy details of Not Mr. T being a total sexist pig in his interview. He played into my hand even better than anticipated. Apparently he'd taken a nap through the school's PR seminar at the beginning of the year.

She was already sitting in Mr. Kavach's room when I rounded the corner. She looked up at me expectantly, but the bell rang for the start of class before we could talk. I eagerly took out a sheet of notebook paper from my bag and did a very un-studious-Savannah thing and decided to pass notes with Grace during class.

I had the interview with Coach Triad this morning!

I slid it under her arm. She opened it immediately, not even trying to be sneaky at this point. She scribbled in her signature purple pen before handing it back to me.

HOW did it go?!

He spilled. Major. I can't wait for you to
listen to the recording.

NO. Way.

Yes way. We're going to be able to blow this
one up, Grace. This is going to be our big
story for the Spartan Spotlight!

And then, Kavach called us out on our not-so-subtle note passing and my brain slipped back into our calculus class.

━━━

After calc I raced to Mrs. Brandt's class to give her the recording of my interview and tell her how well it went. Her eyes lit up when I went over every truth-baring detail that Coach Triad spilled (and made appropriately angry faces for every sexist thing he uttered, too).

"Oh, Savannah, this is going to be a big story," she said, grabbing a piece of notebook paper. "I want you to talk to Chase Stevens. He was a student of mine from about three or four years ago who was approached by recruiters after baseball season. Now that he's done playing college ball I think he'd be willing to talk about what went down without the fear of having it hurt his chances at playing."

"Ooh, that would be perfect," I said. "I'm also going to make a point of getting an interview with the dance team coach, and maybe a few from the past just to confirm the numbers we have on salary. Should we expand it a bit? To other sports? I think the next natural step would be to get the softball team involved, since it's the closest parallel."

"You're on the right track," she said. "But is the story going to be about the disparity between boys' and girls' sports? Because I think that story has been blown in the past."

"No, you're right," I said. "It's totally about the money that is funneling into that program. There's something that isn't adding up."

"Bingo. This is why I keep you around," she said, winking. She handed me the piece of paper with Chase's information on it and smiled down at me. "I'm really proud of you for working so hard on this. You know that this will most likely get pushback from the school, but you're going for it anyway. I hope you're considering a journalism program for school. I could help you identify some standout programs."

I shifted my weight, looking down at the ground. "I think I'm going to Indiana State in the fall. They have a decent program."

She nodded. "I'm not knocking Indiana State, because I have a lot of students who go there and love it, but not all of them have the academic success that you have. Savannah, I really think you should consider applying to places like Columbia and NYU with your test scores and your talent. And you have a very happy teacher who would be willing to write glowing recommendation letters for you."

"That means a lot to me," I said. "I'll think about it."

I put the scrap of paper in my backpack as the last warning bell for second period rang. I now had T minus two minutes to run to the gymnasium and get dressed for PE. It was going to be another one of those days where I got docked points for taking too long to get dressed.

"I've got to get going. I'll keep you updated when I get those interviews scheduled," I said.

"Sounds great!" she called after me.

I didn't understand the guilty feeling that ate a hole into my chest as I left her room. Wasn't it my choice where I wanted to go to school? I'd decided a long time ago that I'd go to whatever school Ashley went to so that we could fulfill our destiny of being the best college roommates ever. Knowing that I had my future planned out so securely was a sense of comfort for me. It helped me get through every fight with Mom, every time my dad canceled his plans to come out and visit us—as long as I could count down the time until I was in college with my best friend again, everything would be okay in the present.

The day went on pretty uneventfully, minus my spectacular fall during a match of Wiffle ball. I definitely put the wiff in Wiffle. I had plans to study with George later, and one could say I was a tad bit excited. We decided it would be easier if we just had a scheduled time to meet each week rather than having to make a new plan all the time. Scheduled George time was very okay with me. I preheated the oven to bake some Toll House breakaway cookies and set them out to prepare them for their grand entrance into the oven and eventually my eager mouth.

The doorbell rang, and I almost skipped to answer it. If I was going to continue to play it cool for George and ignore how dorky-hot he was, I needed to act like a regularly functioning human being in front of him. My uncoordinated skipping was not helping me achieve normal-human status.

"Hey," I said. He stood outside my doorframe with a Pizza Kitchen pepperoni pie in hand, and I don't think I've seen anything more beautiful than George with a pizza. His almost-red hair was sticking out at odd angles, like he'd just woken up from an after-school nap and remembered he needed to be here. My mouth watered (for multiple reasons, mostly the pizza, though, to be honest) and I invited him inside.

"You're seriously an angel for bringing pizza with you," I said. "It's like you finally understand how to get on my good side."

"It's been a long road to get here. Things Savannah doesn't like: three-legged races and almost being hit by a car. Things she does like: pizza."

And you, I wanted to say. Suddenly I felt silly for thinking it. Of course he wasn't interested in me. He was adorable, charming, and actually nice. I was a sometimes-mean and generally unagreeable chubby girl. The reality of that thought stung me for a moment.

"You've learned quickly, grasshopper. I'm quite impressed," I said.

We sat across from each other in silence for a few moments before the oven's preheating alarm went off.

"Oh! I've got to put the cookies in!" I said.

"Did you make me cookies? Now I feel lame for bringing the pizza," he said.

"They're premade Toll House cookies. All I have to do is plop them onto a cookie sheet and put them in the oven. Another thing you will learn quickly is that I'm not the domestic goddess that my mother wishes I was. I can pretty much make mac and cheese and put frozen food in the oven, and that is the extent of my cooking skills," I said.

"I'm still impressed," he said.

Fiyero came up to inspect the pizza box sitting on the table, and George started talking in his dog voice at my fur baby and everything inside of me melted. I don't know what it is about seeing someone you're into interact with your pets that is so heartwarming, but it definitely made me swoon all over George again.

He opened the box of pizza, which was our signature half-pepperoni and half-pineapple. I scooped up a plate from our cabinet and set it in front of him just in time to catch a rogue pineapple from hitting the floor. Fiyero whined at me, knowing that if that pineapple had fallen, he would have had a delicious treat.

"What's the quiz on this week?" I asked, settling into my spot. I grabbed a slice of pepperoni and started eating to my heart's content.

"Polynomial functions," he said, sighing. "You'd think this functions thing would be getting easier after a few weeks of it, but I'm still having the worst time."

"Maybe you haven't had the most qualified tutor in the world," I said, picking off a pepperoni and popping it into my mouth.

"No, you've been great," he said. "At least with your help I can fumble through problems with an inkling of an idea about what's going on. Without you, my precalc grade would be in the toilet."

"Don't beat yourself up too much. You got an A on your last quiz, didn't you?" I asked.

"A pity A. I got extra credit for coming to enough before- and after-school practice sessions with Kavach," he said.

"There's no shame in that game," I said, "And I bet Kavach is way more comfortable giving As to people who actually give a damn about doing well in his class. You've been putting in the effort above and beyond most people."

"Tell me what it's like to be inside your head," he said suddenly.

"Trust me, you don't want to take a look around in there. There's a lot of stuff going on that no one realizes," I said, resting my head in my hand.

"Like what?" he asked.

I looked up at him, gauging how genuinely interested he would be in hearing all my deepest, darkest thoughts. His eyes met mine and never left, never feeling self-conscious about how long we looked at each other. My heart raced at the thought of telling this boy that I'd only met a few weeks ago about myself. He made me feel like I'd known him for years, like we'd put a bookmark in our friendship and we were picking up where we left off. I didn't know whether to be excited or scared that I already felt so comfortable and familiar with him. I decided to stick with excited for my own sanity.

Mom decided now would be the perfect time to shuffle her way back into the kitchen, pausing to look down at me.

"What are you cooking?" she asked.

I turned around, trying to give her the "Please do me a solid and leave us alone" eye, but she didn't register my silent plea.

"Baking," I corrected. "There are cookies in the oven."

She went over to the oven and switched it off, putting on an oven mitt hastily. She took the cookies out and tossed them on the counter.

"Those weren't done!" I said, walking over to her.

"You know how I feel about having processed sugars in this house," she said. Her eyes were wild, like she hadn't slept in days. Her robe hung open to reveal her in a teensy-tiny camisole and shorts, her collarbone jutting out sharply against the robe. I tried to think back to the last time I actually saw her eat in this house, and I couldn't remember.

"I made them for my friend. Remember George? The boy in our kitchen witnessing your freak-out?" I asked.

She started scraping the partially cooked balls of cookie dough into the trash can, disregarding all my yells asking her to stop. She was on her own mission in her mind, and nothing that I was saying could break her out of her daze.

Her eyes snapped to the pizza on the table and she started making her way toward it. I turned to George in horror as she made her way closer to him. This was the final straw. He'd never want to get to know me better after seeing Mom like this. We'd hit our friendship breaking point, and all I could do was watch it happen.

"Stop, Mom, stop!" I yelled. "He brought that; he bought it with his own money! Please stop!"

She stopped slowly, turning back around to face me. Horrified tears had already started falling down my face as I waited for her next move.

"Get it out of my house," she said. "If it's not gone before I get back, you're grounded."

Like a tornado, she exited the room. I was frozen to my spot, never wanting to look at George again. How could I after what he just saw? Anxiety sprouted from my toes and wound itself up my body like unwanted ivy on a building. When it reached my lungs, the force of it made me hitch forward. I held on to my chest in an effort to keep myself together at all costs.

George touched my shoulder tentatively, and I looked up at him. I tried to wipe my eyes quickly so that he wouldn't notice I was crying, but it was too late. He'd seen the stream of tears already. Every part of me expected him to come up with an excuse to leave, any way for him to get out of this awful situation, but instead he asked the question that I didn't realize I needed to hear the most.

"Are you okay?" he asked.

I shook my head, not able to hold back the tears anymore. He wrapped me up into a hug and held my head to his shoulder. He didn't try to analyze the situation or give any advice. He just held me as I cried. My hands locked themselves together behind his back, and in this moment I felt safer than I had in a long time. Here, like this, Mom's words couldn't hurt me. The neglect from my dad over the past two years was a distant memory. With George I was able to forget all the ickiness that had become my life and be supremely content, even if it was just for a few moments.

"Let's get out of here," he said. I nodded into his chest before pulling away. I wiped under my eyes to catch the makeup that made liquid trails down my cheeks.

"Oh, shoot," I said, pulling on his shirt, which now had a mascara stain on it.

"Don't worry about it," he said. He picked up the pizza box, and I rested a quick kiss on Fiyero's head before heading off, trying to silently apologize to him for leaving him alone with Mom for a while.

We piled into his mom's car and he turned up the radio on full blast. It happened to be one of Pitbull's latest hits, and George timed his signature "Dale!" in perfect unison with Mr. Worldwide. I burst out laughing at how ridiculous it was that George could sing every word to a Pitbull song and be incredibly funny after what he just witnessed. God, I needed the laugh.

The road twisted into the route to Sandcastle Park, the place where we'd had our eventful meeting for the first time. Today it was pretty empty—everyone must be busy on this Monday afternoon. That, or they heard our fight across town and everyone collectively decided that I needed some time in Sandcastle Park more than they did.

He led me to the playground that had a castle tower at the top of the slide. It had been an ongoing debate between Ashley and me whether the castle tower came before the naming of the park. It was a classic chicken-or-the-egg debacle. I liked to believe the castle slide inspired the name, since it was one of my favorite places in the entire park.

He sat down on one of the swings, and I joined him, swaying back and forth.

"Whenever I'm angry, when I feel like I could explode with all my nervous energy, I swing. And, since I'm new to town and don't know any other parks besides this one, these are the swings of choice," he said.

He started pumping his legs, and I followed him. Once we were high enough off the ground, I started to lean backward each time I went forward. There was a certain type of power in being able to manipulate when your blood rushed to your head. I felt in control of how my body was feeling in a way that I didn't normally.

He let out a high-pitched yell as he reached the peak of his height of the swing and I thought it would break off from going so high. But he came down.

"Try it!" he yelled.

I let out a little scream, testing the waters.

"Louder!" he said.

This time my yell echoed around the park. As I let it out, I felt like a weight had lifted off my chest. The horrible energy that had been cooped up inside of me for weeks was let out in that one yell, and I felt free. I tipped my head back, relishing in my new weightless feeling. It was pretty damn glorious.

George leaped from his swing, landing feetfirst on the mulch in front of us. I let the height of my swing die down a bit before I attempted my jump, knowing that I'd probably break an ankle if I attempted the same jump as him.

He sat down on the picnic table across from the swings, where he'd set the pizza down. He opened the box back open and took out a slice, taking a big bite into it. I sat down across from him and rested my head in my hands. He kicked my shin under the table and motioned toward a slice of pizza, and I shook my head. I'd lost my appetite.

"I'm sorry you had to see that back there," I said.

"Stop," he said. "Seriously, we don't have to talk about it."

"I'm so embarrassed," I said.

He tapped my foot with his until I looked back up to meet his eyes. "Every family has stuff. Don't be embarrassed."

"It's just—the only person who has ever seen her like that is Grace, but she's known us forever. She knew Mom before she changed and knows that whatever *that* was, wasn't her. You didn't know her before, and it makes me so sad that this is the Mom that you get to meet," I said.

"You mean before the TV show?" he asked.

"Yeah," I said, breaking eye contact with him. "Well, before my dad cheated on her, really. Things started spiraling pretty quickly after that."

"That . . . that sucks," George said.

"I always wished that I'd been born into Grace's family, ever since I was little. She and Mrs. M have this amazing relationship, and Mr. and Mrs. M love the hell out of each other, and they always make all this time to be a family—I never realized how bad things were with our family until I went over to Grace's house," I said.

"What about your sister?" George asked.

"Ashley has been the one saving grace of everything happening in our family. She is the one who always held us all together, mostly the one who held me together. She's the perfect opposite to me, calm, caring, and protective to my outspoken, stubborn, and opinionated," I said.

"You say opinionated and outspoken like they're bad things," he said.

"Those two traits have gotten me in the most trouble over the years," I said.

"Savannah, of course you're outspoken and opinionated—you've got so much stored up inside your brain that it would be impossible for you to keep it quiet," he said.

I blushed a deep red all over. "Can I appoint you as my official hype man? Can you just follow me around at all times and spin all my bad traits into good ones?"

"Sign me up." He smiled. His brown eyes crinkled in the corners, and I wanted so badly to reach out and kiss him in this moment. I'd never felt that desire so strongly in my life before, that I needed to attach his face to mine or I would pass out right here in Sandcastle Park. I sat on my hands to keep from reaching out toward him involuntarily. I had no idea what my body was capable of with this overwhelming feeling taking over me.

"So," he said, breaking me out of my daze. "I have this competition that I have to perform at for jazz band on Friday. I'm not sure if you like jazz or if you're even into that sort of thing, but I wanted to extend the invite just in case—"

"I'll be there," I said. "Just tell me when and where and I'll for sure be there."

His blush was matching mine from earlier, and we both smiled like big dummies at each other. I tapped his foot under the table like he had done with mine earlier and he met my eyes again.

"Thank you," I said.

"Don't mention it," he replied.

From that moment, I decided that a blushing George was my new favorite thing to look at.

chapter TEN

I snuck out of the house before Mom had a chance to wake up and see me leave. I didn't bother to leave a note. After the last few days, I figured she didn't particularly care where I'd gone.

George texted me that their competition was at Merrill Middle School, a school from the county over. He was competing in two events—one with the full jazz band from the high school and one combo. The performance with the whole band was first, and I followed the Sharpie signs to the auditorium. I grabbed a program on the way into the auditorium and found a seat in the back, not in the biggest people mood at the moment.

I scanned the program until I found George's name, and it sent a little shiver of excitement down my spine. I didn't realize how excited I was to see him play until that moment.

"Next we have the Springdale band under the direction of Dr. Rauch," someone announced from the side of the stage. George walked onto the stage with his saxophone in hand, his mess of strawberry blond curls tamed by an extreme amount of gel. It was weird seeing him in a shirt buttoned all the way to the top and dress shoes. I preferred his signature sneakers any day.

They started things off with a bang, George bouncing in time with the beat as he played. They all seemed to take their cues off him—each time he would breathe in they would start in on a new phrase. It was a choreographed dance that George was the center of. He stood up in the middle of the song to stand in front of the microphone at the front of the stage. He closed his eyes and started to solo, riffing off the band behind him. He never missed a beat, even though it was completely made up on the spot. When he finished, his face spread into his signature lopsided smile before he went back to join the band again. I let out an extra loud "Go, George!" in the mixture of the audience's applause.

The set was over all too soon, and everyone who came to watch Springdale started to file out of the auditorium. I waited until most people had left before I got up from my seat, looking at the program to see where his combo would be performing next.

"Savannah?" someone asked when I left the auditorium.

I looked up to find a young girl who looked a little

bit like Grace, if Grace had blue eyes and was still thirteen years old.

"I'm Hannah," she said. "George's sister. He showed me your picture on Instagram, sorry if that's creepy."

"Not creepy at all," I said, blushing just thinking about Hannah taking a spin through my Instagram feed. Thirteen-year-olds were a thousand times cooler on Instagram with their themes and what not. I wondered what she thought about my series of "hot dog or leg?" photos from last year. Ashley and I got a good laugh from them at least.

"We're about to head over to his combo if you want to come sit with us?" she asked, motioning toward her parents standing in the middle of the Merrill Middle School lobby. Mrs. Smith waved at me and showed me the same lopsided smile that I'd come to recognize as George's.

"Sure, that would be great," I said.

"Mom, Dad, this is Savannah. George's . . ." Hannah trailed off.

"Friend," I interjected, holding out my hand. "I'm George's friend Savannah."

"It's so nice to meet you, Savannah," Mrs. Smith said. "George has told us so much about you. It's been really nice for him to have such a great friend as he transitions to his new school. Thank you for that."

"Oh, no, he's definitely helped me out more than I've helped him. Trust me," I said.

"We have a few minutes before he performs again," Mr. Smith said, checking his watch. I loved that he still wore a watch and checked it rather than using his phone.

"Let's get scootin'!" Mrs. Smith said.

We made our way down the hallway, and Hannah caught up to my side as we walked.

"Let's send a good-luck Snap to George before he goes on!" she said, positioning the camera so that we were both in the frame of her selfie. She put up a thumbs-up in the picture and all I could do was attempt to smile before she pulled the phone away.

"I think I blinked, should we redo it?" I asked.

"You look cute, don't worry," she said. Commence the full-body blush on my part.

The room that we went in to watch the combo was a much smaller classroom where you could most definitely see the audience watching you. I sat down in the front row, in between Hannah and Mrs. Smith, as we waited for the combo to come into the room.

"It was very nice of you to come, Savannah," Mrs. Smith said. "I know it will mean a lot to George."

"I've been dying to see him play. I wouldn't miss it," I said.

A girl walked into the room with a sheet of paper in her hand. Her hands shook nervously as she read from it. "Next we have the Springdale swing combo from Springdale High."

This time when George walked into the room, his eyes found mine immediately. His smile grew across his face, and damn, it was pretty contagious. I couldn't control the smile that crossed my lips and stayed plastered there for the rest of the performance.

George counted everyone off, fully in the leadership position now that there wasn't a director standing in front of them. He moved his body more during this performance, almost being the conductor with just his body movements. This music seemed more challenging and quick, and I watched in awe as his fingers moved deftly over the keys. I wondered how many hours of practice it took to perfect these songs, let alone the practice with the whole combo to make sure that everyone's parts fit together seamlessly.

As the combo hit their last note, I instantly started clapping and even let out an embarrassingly loud *whoop*! Was it not customary to whoop at a jazz band concert? I didn't care. I was all kinds of impressed and proud, and the whoop was the best way that I knew to show it.

"Georgie said he'd meet us in the lobby," Mrs. Smith said, patting my leg. I followed them back down and waited anxiously to see George. I had so many questions for him. How did he become appointed the leader? What did they call it when he held out that really high and impressive note for a long time? How was he so confident when he performed solos? How did he know he wouldn't mess up? So. Many. Questions.

Mr. Suave Saxophone Man rounded the corner with his case about ten minutes later after Hannah had the perfect amount of time to suggest an Instagram theme for me to start using. Mrs. Smith wrapped him in a giant congratulatory hug before he could acknowledge the rest of his posse, and my heart squeezed when she planted a big kiss on his cheek. When he pulled away from her, he looked at me. My breath left my lungs in a whoosh, and I swear for two seconds I could hear my heart beating in my ears.

He walked over to me, and we stood in this awkward, do-we-or-don't-we-hug limbo that was doing unfair things to my nerve endings. I settled on crossing my arms in front of my chest and smiling up at him rather than going in for the unreciprocated hug.

"You were amazing up there," I said. "I didn't know that I was tutoring a music prodigy."

"Prodigy's a little bit of a stretch," he said, rubbing his hand on the back of his neck. His telltale nervous sign.

"No, seriously, you were amazing. And they all just followed you whenever you'd move—it was kind of incredible.

How come I never knew that jazz band was such a big deal at Springdale?" I asked.

"You've obviously been hanging out with the wrong crowd," he said. "But seriously, thank you for coming. It, uh, it means a lot to me."

"Of course," I said. I wanted so badly to reach out and grab his hand that wasn't currently occupied by his saxophone case. We were both smiling at each other for an unknown amount of time before Mr. Smith coughed behind us. We both turned around quickly and knew that my face was turning red.

"Savannah, would you like to come over for dinner? I'm making some celebratory homemade spaghetti and meatballs. Unless you're vegetarian. We can go meatball-less, too!" she said.

"Oh, no, I'm a big fan of meatballs," I said. Hannah started snickering from her phone, and George sent her a warning look. Truthfully, it was taking everything inside of me to not laugh at the innuendo I just dropped in front of my crush's parents, too.

"Well, great! George, why don't you drive back with Savannah to show her the way to our house, okay? We'll meet you both back there!"

Hannah waggled her eyebrows at us as she left with their parents. Once they rounded the corner I burst out laughing.

"Subtlety is not one of my family's greatest strengths," he said.

"I see," I said, recovering from my laughing attack. "Norma's this way."

"Norma?" he asked.

"Did I not explain that my beloved car is named Norma?" I asked.

"You would name your car," he said.

"She needs a name for when I accidentally hit the curb and I have to apologize to her," I said.

"Obviously. How silly of me to think that you wouldn't name her something."

He flung his saxophone case in the back seat and climbed into the passenger seat. We had about fifteen minutes of a car ride ahead of us, and I was already thinking of all the conversation starters that I had in my back pocket.

"So Hannah is going to help me start an Instagram theme," I said. "She thinks I look like a blue-tint kind of girl. What do you think?"

"I think I don't understand Instagram," he said.

"Thank God I'm not the only one," I said.

His leg was bouncing up and down nervously, and I tried to focus on the road in front of me to forget that a very cute and talented George was sitting in my front seat.

"I just—"

"When did—"

We both started at the same time.

"You go," I said.

"Oh, okay," he said. "I was going to ask when you got there. Did you see the first performance?"

"I did! I was in the back; you probably couldn't see me," I said.

"That was probably for the best," he said. "I was a lot less nervous because I didn't know you were there."

"I made you nervous?" I asked.

"Well, yeah," he said. "I got that Snapchat from Hannah, and I thought I might be sick!"

"Wait, what? Why? You were so good!" I said.

"I mean, you're so good at everything you do. I wanted to prove that I was kind of sort of good at something, too," he said. He looked out the window as he finished his sentence, and I felt my mouth drop open.

"George, what's your middle name?" I asked.

"Samuel."

"George Samuel Smith, do you even realize how wonderful you are?" I asked. "Do you need an official hype woman? Because I'm your gal if you need one."

"You think I'm wonderful?" he asked.

"Yes. Now we've hit our cheesy quota for this car ride. I will literally ooze cheese if we praise each other anymore. Here's the aux cord. Pick out something fun to play," I said.

He put on Eminem, and I burst out laughing as he started rapping all of "Lose Yourself." If I didn't know any better, I'd say he practiced it. And that fact made my heart soar.

We somehow made it back to his house before the rest of his family, and he led me inside. There were still a few boxes piled up in the living room, but adorable pictures of baby George and Hannah hung on the walls. I stopped to look at all of them, my particular favorite being one of two-year-old George in a bath filled with rubber ducks.

"I need to go drop this upstairs. Do you want to come up?" he asked.

"George Samuel Smith, are you asking me to go to your bedroom with you?" I asked in my best Southern belle accent.

"It's a regular town scandal," he said, leading me up the stairs.

His bedroom was fairly plain, with a double bed pushed into one corner of the room and with sheet music scattered all over the floor. The walls were still bare, like he'd just managed to set up the bed and then gave up on unpacking the rest of his things.

"I was expecting more posters of naked video game characters," I said.

"I keep it nerdy chic in my room, thank you very much," he said.

He pulled his normal uniform of a T-shirt and jeans from a pile of clothes on the floor and turned to leave. "I'll be back in a sec."

"You can change in here, I'll promise to close my eyes," I said.

"Do you think Clark Kent ever let people stay in the same room when he became Superman? I can't possibly have you know my secrets."

"I guess you're right. Go on, Clark," I said.

He shuffled out of the room and into the bathroom. I sat down on the edge of his bed, taking in the mess of it all. I suddenly became acutely aware that I was in George's bedroom while his parents weren't home. What would the casual onlooker think? Would they think we were a couple? Or would they think that I'd been hopelessly friend-zoned by the supercute saxophone boy?

When I looked back to the left, George was leaning against his doorframe with his arms crossed. My heart beat wildly in my ears, and I wished so badly that he would close the distance between us and kiss me. We stared at each other for three beats before we heard the sound of the garage door go up.

"And that's our cue," he said, not breaking eye contact.

I slowly stood up and followed him back downstairs to the promise of Mrs. Smith's delicious spaghetti and meatballs.

When we made our way back downstairs, Mrs. Smith was already boiling pasta and heating up the most delicious-smelling sauce ever on the stove. Hannah and Mr. Smith were sitting in the living room, starting a questionable Netflix movie that neither of them had heard of before. Those were the true gambles in life.

"We can chitchat in the kitchen, if you'd like!" Mrs. Smith said over her shoulder.

George and I took a seat at two matching stools at their kitchen counter while she worked at the stove, adding dashes of spice and a little bit of water here and there to her sauce.

"So, Savannah, George tells me you're a mathematician," she said.

"Oh, not really," I said. "I just like calculus."

"Well, you've been really helpful to George. He's always struggled with math," she said.

"Thanks, Mom," George said, a blush creeping up on his cheeks.

"Sorry! Sorry! Foot in mouth," she said.

"So, do you or your husband play music?" I asked.

"Oh, gosh no! But my sister plays clarinet. Georgie started on the clarinet, did you know that?" she asked.

I turned to face him, raising my eyebrows. "I didn't know that."

"It's pretty standard for saxes to start on clarinet," he said.

"He teaches lessons on saxophone and clarinet," Mrs. Smith said.

"Ma," he started.

"What? I'm proud of you, that's all!" she said. "I don't know why you two in there started a movie. Dinner is going to be ready here in a second!"

Hannah and Mr. Smith grumbled from the other room before getting up and coming to the kitchen. It's like they all had some unspoken roles in the dinner process that they all fulfilled. Each of the Smiths went to different parts of the kitchen to grab plates, silverware, cups, and placemats and set them out accordingly. I watched their silent dance in awe, wondering if this was how normal four-person families functioned. The only other family besides my own that I had to base it on was Grace's, but she lived in a six-person household, which was decidedly more chaotic than most.

"Savannah, why don't you come serve yourself, dear!" Mrs. Smith said, handing me a plate. I looked in to the pot of delicious carb-ridden goodness and my mouth watered. We hadn't eaten regular noodles in the house in over a year, and the sight and smell of them made me practically drool on my plate. Good-bye forever, spiralized zucchini noodles.

I took a heaping helping with me to the table and poured myself a glass of water before sitting down. I loved that their table was actually in the kitchen and not removed in a dining room somewhere. You were right in the action, and it made everything and everyone seem so much closer and more involved.

Their family chatted animatedly throughout the whole meal (dropping some bread crumbs of amazing embarrassing stories of George along the way) and not once did one of them monitor the other person's meal. I knew that I was stuffed to the brim from all the spaghetti that I grabbed the first time, but knowing that I would have the option to go back up for a second round of food without any judgment made the biggest sense of relief and calm fall over me.

———

Spending time with George and his amazing family made me realize how incredibly angry and tired I was of the way that Mom had been treating me lately. Sure, she'd been dealing with her own issues surrounding seeing herself on *Shake the Weight* again for the first time in six months, but she had no right to completely go off the wall while my friend was over. It was one thing to be controlling about what I ate, but it was a whole other thing to be controlling over what George ate or brought into the house.

Her car was still in the driveway when I pulled up. Good. Now would finally be the time that I let go of all the anger that I'd held back in an effort to keep the peace between us. All the pent-up anger in the last few weeks started to well inside of me, and I knew that once I saw her face, I could quite possibly explode.

My anger ricocheted inside my chest as I made my way through the front door. I could hear the pitter-patter of her feet hitting the floor in her room, the telltale sign of her doing a jump rope workout. I flew up the stairs, not entirely sure what I would say first. I wasn't always in my best form off the cuff, but I knew that if I didn't say something now, I never would have the guts.

The door smacked against the wall of her bedroom and she let out a small yelp, turning to face me.

"I didn't hear you come home," she said. "You scared the daylights out of me."

"Oh, I scared you? How about you scaring me yesterday?" I said.

"What do you mean?" she asked.

"When George was over and you went all Godzilla on my baking session," I said.

"I don't know what you want me to say, Savannah.

I've told you numerous times that I don't want that kind of food in my house, and you explicitly disobeyed that rule," she said.

"I had a friend over. He brought the food. It was a completely different situation," I said.

She wiped her forehead with a towel that she'd slung across the end of her bed and took a sip from her water bottle before turning back to face me.

"You'd be a lot happier if you could just make the choice to lead a healthier life. I have a goal to work toward. When I'm down another fifteen pounds, I can fit back into my swimsuit and go swimming again. How wonderful will that be?" she asked.

"You are perfectly capable of going swimming right now with the body you have right now," I said.

"Not the way that I want to go swimming," she said.

"And what happens if you don't lose those fifteen pounds? Will you never swim again?" I asked.

Her hands flew into the air in an angry spiral. "Don't put that kind of negativity out into the universe, Savannah. I'm going to lose those fifteen pounds and be happier because of it."

"So what happens when you do drop those fifteen pounds? Will you be content? When is this going to stop, Mom? When there's nothing left of you?" I asked.

"Don't talk to me like that. You think you know what's best for everyone around you? I am in control of my body—not you, not your father—no one," she snapped.

I flinched. "I'm just worried about you," I said quietly, my resolve starting to crumble.

I could sense her pulling away into herself. All the anger that I'd had earlier was slowly turning into fear. Fear for the look in her eyes while she screamed about having control of her body. Fear for the circles that were prominently showing under her eyes. Fear for the bones that were more pronounced in her figure than the last time I looked at her.

"I wish you'd stop worrying so much about me and start worrying about yourself. I'm sorry that I tried to save you from processed sugar and fatty foods. Excuse me for wanting my daughter to have a better life than I did growing up when I was—"

"Fat?" I finished for her. I felt the tears sting in my eyes as I tried to keep my voice steady. "News flash: *fat* isn't a bad word, Mom. It's the twenty-first century. I have blue eyes. I have blond hair. I'm fat. Literally nothing about my life is changed because that word is associated with my physical appearance. I'm sorry that someone taught you to hate yourself because of your body somewhere along the way, but I'm not going to let you pull me down with you."

"Savannah—" she started.

"No. I've said what I had to say. And until you are ready to have a real conversation about this, I have to go."

And, in a completely un-Savannah-like fashion, I raced down the stairs, snatching my car keys as I stormed out the front door.

chapter ELEVEN

The last place I wanted to be was home alone with Mom. I calculated in my head how long of a drive it would be to get to Indiana State and decided that the only way I would be able to sleep that night was if I was with Ashley. Despite my ever-present fear of driving, especially at night, I went against my better judgment and hopped inside Norma the Nissan.

I convinced myself that as long as I was listening to Brendon Urie's voice—he was the soundtrack to the movie that was my life—there was no way that he'd let me crash. I would make it in one piece to Ashley's dorm room by the power of Panic! at the Disco and she would make everything better.

Forty-five minutes on the interstate went by surprisingly quickly. I was about a half hour out from Indiana State and signs for Terre Haute were starting to pop up alongside the car. I'd distracted myself by loudly singing along to the CD in the car, especially when giant trucks would get themselves into my safety bubble in between cars. I kept telling myself that one more song finished was another five minutes closer to Ashley, to having someone tell me that everything was going to be okay.

The Indiana State University exit came into view and my heart swelled. I had finally made it with Norma, still all intact. I wound through the campus, only kind of remembering how to get to her dorm building from the day when we dropped her off. Thankfully there were signs pointing to Reeve Hall. I parked behind the dorm building, hoping that it would only warrant a cheap ticket and that they wouldn't tow Norma away. Either way, it was too late to find their free parking, and Norma was staying right where I left her.

I followed a group of girls through the door of Ashley's dorm and got onto the elevator behind them, hitting the tenth-floor button. God, I hoped she was home by now. It didn't even register with me that it was a Friday night and that she was probably out at a party with friends. What if she went home with someone for the night and never came back to her room? Would I have to sleep out in the hallway like a weirdo?

I approached room 1014 slowly, hovering my fist just above the door. I should have called. Coming without warning was not what Ashley deserved, especially if she was making new friends and having new experiences. Still, here I was.

I knocked anyway. I held my breath until I heard the lock click open. The door swung open to an Ashley in her pj's with her hair sticking to one side of her face. The lights were off, and she rubbed her eyes, double-taking at seeing me in her doorframe.

"Savannah?" she asked, her voice with a slight lisp from her nighttime retainers.

"Hi," I said, my voice cracking.

"Oh my God, what happened?" she asked. "Come in. Come here."

She pulled me into a bear hug, and my head rested in the crook of her neck. I couldn't believe that I was here actually seeing her again. I felt like it had been lifetimes since we had seen each other, and not just a week. I wasn't sure how anyone did this whole "being a sibling but living far away from each other" thing. At least for me, it was turning out to be pretty rough.

She separated us to be at arm's length so she could look at me. I held back tears in an extreme way, wanting to seem like I was more together than I actually was. But who was I kidding? She knew that something bad had to have happened for me to make the drive in the dark.

"What happened?" she asked, more firmly this time. She

led me to the futon underneath Isabel's lofted bed and turned on the fairy lights that wound along the legs and underneath the bed.

"On Monday, Mom had a huge freak-out at me about food," I said. "Like, she was the most out of it that I'd ever seen her. I had been making cookies for George and me to eat while we were studying, and she comes down and takes them out of the oven while they're still baking and starts throwing the half-baked cookies in the trash while she keeps yelling at me about processed sugar. All in front of George. It was absolutely mortifying."

"Oh my God," she said. "Savvy, something has to be wrong with her."

"We've known this for months, Ashley! That show messed with her brain. But 'we're the kids' and we can't tell her that we're scared by how she's acting or that we think she should get help," I said. "I don't know what to do, Sissy. I don't want to be home alone with her anymore. I'm scared," I said.

She looked across the room, her brain calculating everything that she could do to make the situation better. This was classic Ashley, trying to fix everyone else's problems so that everyone around her could be happy. I didn't know if there was anything that she could do herself to fix this one. It was almost too far gone for us to handle on our own.

"You can absolutely stay for tonight and tomorrow

night. We'll figure out a way tomorrow for you to stay with Grace for the next couple of nights until things get figured out. I could come home for a while until things blow over, or if they blow up, I'll be there to handle it with you," she said.

"You can't just leave school," I said.

"It would only be for a few days," she said.

As much as I would love for her to come back home and act as a buffer to Mom's newfound episodes, she couldn't start coming home so soon in school. If she came back and realized how far gone things were, she wouldn't want to go back to school. And that wasn't fair to her. She deserved to be in college and have her new group of friends and be happy.

"No, I'll figure it out with Grace. I think you should stay here. Learn how to be a full-fledged adult and stuff," I said.

"Savvy—"

"Not up for debate," I said. I took her hands in mine and faced her. "But I will one thousand percent stay here tonight. There's no way in hell I'm getting back in that car and driving in the dark."

"I can't believe you drove all the way here. Is this the longest you've ever taken Norma for a spin?" she asked.

"Yes, and I never want to do it again," I said, leaning back into the futon. I could finally relax my muscles that had been tense from the moment I got into the car. The exhaustion from the night finally set in, and I wasn't sure that I could get up from the futon.

"What did George say?" she asked.

"What?" I asked, my eyes popping open.

"When he saw Mom like that. How did he react?" she asked.

"He was super cool about it. Lovely, even. He made me feel like it was just a normal thing that he was used to seeing," I said.

"He sounds like he's a good person to have in your corner," she said.

"He is," I replied.

"Will I ever get to meet the illustrious George?" she asked.

"I hope so," I said, leaning my head against the arm of the futon. "He's kind of wonderful. He makes up for a lot of the shitty things that have been going down with Mom lately."

"Well, good. You deserve to have a George in your life. Shall we toast with a pint of unopened ice cream?" she asked.

"You have spoken my language," I said.

Thankfully, Ashley had the wherewithal to text Mom that I was there with Norma that night before I passed out on the futon. The combination of being entirely exhausted from the day's events, plus the ice cream right before bed, put me into a deep sleep that I didn't wake up from until around noon on Saturday. I could hear Ashley and her roommate, Isabel, whispering about why I was here unannounced. Isabel made Ashley promise that she wouldn't have unannounced visitors again. There's guilt bomb number one thousand for this weekend.

Once Isabel was gone, I peeked my eyes open. I rolled over to look at Ashley, who was sprawled out on the floor reading a textbook.

"I'm sorry if I pissed your roommate off," I said.

"Don't be," she said. "If she's weirded out by my sister spending the night, we've got bigger issues."

"What's the plan for the day?" I asked. For the first time I realized what a bad idea it was to travel to my sister's college dorm room without a change of clothes or a toothbrush. I felt grimy and gross from the day before without any way to remedy that situation.

"Well, first we need to go have the amazing dining hall brunch that they cook on the weekends. It's like they know that greasy breakfast food will cure all our hangovers the next day," she said.

"I'm always down for some greasy breakfast," I said.

"Then I thought we could shop around town a little

bit. There are cute stores, especially the local bookstore, that I think you would like. And then tonight, if you're up for it, we could go to a party I'm planning on going to and you could meet my friends. They practically know you at this point, because I talk about you all the time," she said.

"You talk about me with your friends?" I asked. I thought that while she'd been off making new friends at school that I was the furthest thing from her mind. It warmed my little sad heart to hear that I was still someone she told her friends about.

"Well, duh," she said. She stood up from her textbook and went in front of her closet. "I actually think I accidentally packed something of yours that was mixed with my laundry when I left. Can you wear these jeans with one of my shirts?"

"I was wondering where those went!" I said.

"Sorry," she said sheepishly. "I've totally been hoarding them."

She tossed me the jeans and a flouncy baby doll top with pink polka dots. Not really my style, but I would take anything to get out of this dress and not have this smell clinging to me anymore. I pulled the top over my head, and even though it was arguably one of Ashley's flowiest tops, it was tight across my chest and my upper arms. I would have to be careful how I moved in it so that I didn't accidentally tear a hole in it.

We moved with a wave of students who also woke up late from a night out. They were all migrating toward the dining hall to get this magical brunch food that Ashley had hyped so much. Honestly, if this doesn't beat out IHOP with all that buildup, I was going to be super disappointed.

When we got inside the dining hall, the line wound around the entire front lobby. I'd never seen so many kids around my age who looked, well, terrible. Everyone looked like they'd rolled out of bed without brushing their hair or bothering to clean off the smudged makeup from their night out. And the best part about it? Literally no one cared. I could get used to that aspect of college.

I heaped a tower of pancakes and hash browns onto my plate without being bothered if they all got drenched in syrup. Even though it was buffet style, I felt like I needed to grab everything I saw that looked delicious before all the hungover college kids got to it first.

After we finished up brunch (totally worth the hype) Ashley took me on a tour of the college town and the little bookstore just off campus like she'd promised. The way she described everything, like she'd lived here forever and with an excited sparkle in her eye, stirred a feeling inside me that was bittersweet. I was happy that she was acclimating to her new life, and that she'd found the people and places that made her happy within it, but I felt like I was no longer part of this equation.

We wandered our way into a coffee shop packed with students huddled around their laptops and heaps of textbooks. I overheard a girl ordering in front of us ask for three shots of espresso, and someone whisper behind her "been there." Midterms were just around the corner, and more guilt started to fill my body. If I wasn't here, Ashley could have been using this time to study.

"Why don't you go find us a table?" Ashley asked, looking around to locate an empty seat. "Is caramel macchiato still your drink?"

"It sure is," I said.

I wound through the mass of overcaffeinated and under-rested college students until I spotted the last free table in the back corner. It was a tall table, which was less than ideal for a short person like myself. I knew just from the look of it that my feet would most definitely fall asleep, because my toes would not be able to reach the bar on the bottom of the chair.

I pulled on the shirt that Ashley let me borrow so that it would come down to cover my backside. I felt like an intruder coming to spy in Ashley's territory, wearing her clothes, sitting in her favorite coffee shop, observing her classmates in their natural habitat. No matter how many times she repeated that it was not a problem that I dropped by unannounced, I still felt like I was ruining her weekend.

"Look, they even made you a coffee heart," Ashley said, sliding the most delicious-looking caramel macchiato that I'd ever seen in front of me. I grasped the giant blue cup, which was truly as big as a cereal bowl, and took my first sip. Glorious. Ashley waited with wide eyes for my official review.

"I heart this so much," I said.

"I knew you would! This is my late-night fuel of choice," she said, finally taking her seat across from me.

"We'll have to go back to that cute little boutique and grab the rhubarb pear perfume for you. My treat," I said.

"Your treat? What secret lottery did you win?" she asked.

"I'll have you know that I'm very judicious with my birthday and holiday money," I said. "Plus, I still have a bunch of cash saved up from that summer we thought detasseling corn was a good idea."

Ashley visibly shuddered. "Never again."

"My hands will never be the same," I said. "But we did make so much bank."

She took a sip from her cup/cereal bowl (undoubtedly a mocha latte, the least coffee-filled drink of all the coffee drinks) and her eyes rolled back in her head. When she set her cup back down, she had a mustache of whipped cream that she wiped off with the sleeve of her shirt.

"How do you feel this morning?" she asked.

We were finally breaking out of our casual normalcy for the day to address the elephant in the room: my personal and emotional breakdown from last night. We'd been coasting along through the day like nothing had happened, and part of me wished that we could just forget the reason that I'd come knocking on her door and spend the day blissfully unaware.

"I'm really okay," I said, shifting in my seat. I adjusted one of my legs underneath me on the chair to prevent it from falling asleep.

"You don't have to pretend with me," she said. "It's okay not to be okay."

"It's just . . . ," I started. How did I even put how I felt into words that made any sense? Even to Ashley, the number one Savannahspeak translator?

"I just feel like, there's this whole community of people in my real life and online who have shown me that I'm allowed to be comfortable and happy in my own body. And I feel that way most times. Most days I can brush off little comments that Mom makes, but some days, they tear me down and negate every positive thing that I've learned to love about myself. It's like no matter how many positive affirmations I get from an article, book, online forum, or human in real life, one comment from her can erase them all. Why does she have so much power over me?" I asked.

"Because you let her," she said. She made it seem so simple. Like taking the power back from the one person I had to live with every day was some easy thing that I could choose to do.

"How do I stop it?" I asked.

Ashley took a long sip from her drink, setting down her cup with careful purpose. She reached out across the table and took my hand in hers.

"You're talking to the person who alienated one side of her family by coming out. For the first year that Grandma and Grandpa Alverson stopped inviting us to things until my 'phase' was over, I was wrecked. You remember that time. It made me hate Thanksgiving and Christmas, which were my absolute favorite holidays. But one day, I woke up and realized that I could keep being miserable about their decision to exclude me for something I had no control over, or I could hope that one day, their desire to get to know their granddaughter and be a part of her life would outweigh their biases," she said.

"But it's been three years now," I said.

Her head sunk a bit, but she squeezed my hand.

"There's no expiration date on acceptance. I do believe

that. Humans have been notoriously stubborn in their beliefs for centuries, but change happens. People evolve. And I'm able to continue on as my true self, living a happy and open life, with the hope that the people I love will come to accept me for who I am eventually," she said. "Give Mom time. She's very wrapped up in her own experience right now, but it won't always be this way."

"How did you get so mature?" I asked.

"Didn't you hear? I'm in college now." She winked.

Ashley's friend Mallory came over to get ready for the party, and they were both taking sips from a bottle of wine they'd snuck into the dorm room. Every part of that sentence made me all sorts of uncomfortable. I may not be an actual student at ISU yet, but I did know that it was against the rules to have alcohol in your room. And that you could be fined quite a bit of money for breaking that rule.

I'd slipped back into the dress I wore last night but doused it in two different kinds of perfume to take away some of the smell of last night's travels that still clung to it. I fishtail-braided my hair again, this time more out of necessity to hide how greasy my hair had become. There was not enough baby powder in the world to make my hair look clean.

"So will Ms. Yael be joining us tonight?" Mallory asked.

Ashley poked her in the side with her elbow. "She said she'd think about it. Nothing was confirmed."

"What?" I said, standing up from the futon. This was some news that I needed to get in on.

"Yael and your lovely sister finally had their rom-com moment two nights ago. I mean, we'd all called it since the first day of classes, but it officially happened," Mallory said.

"I knew that you two would be a thing!" I said.

"We aren't a 'thing' and nothing is official. Y'all are jinxing it! Just let me bask in the fact that it happened and I'll go from there," she said.

I came up behind her and wrapped her in a hug. "I'm so happy for you. You deserve a rom-com moment."

"Thanks, Sissy," she said, wrapping her arms around mine. She went back to getting ready with Mallory, and I watched it all unfold like a fly on the wall. If I weren't here, she'd probably get to a good buzz off the wine and build up the confidence to go over and ask Yael to go with her to the party. She would say yes (because who could say no to Ashley?) and they would go to the party and have many more rom-com moments together. It would be the perfect, fun weekend for her and a chance to explore the new possibility of a relationship with Yael.

But instead she was here, having to include her high school sister who was in a less-than-happy spot. I'd intruded on her plans for the weekend without asking and without taking into consideration that she might not want me to be there. I wrapped my arms around my legs on the futon as Mallory and Ashley finished getting ready. When Ashley turned to me, I motioned toward the door.

"You guys go out and have fun. Please, go make sure that that girl goes to that party with you. You'll have way more fun with her than you will with your sober high school sister. I'm super tired anyway—I might just crash in your bed until you come home," I said.

"What? No! You should come to the party! It will be fun, I promise. Even if you're sober," she said.

"I love you for wanting to include me, but seriously. You should go have a fun time and don't worry about me. I'll be out once my head hits the pillow. I promise," I said.

"Are you sure?" she asked.

"Positive," I said. "But the only promise you have to make me is that you will make sure that Yael goes out with you tonight in my absence."

"Ugh," she sighed. "I guess that can be arranged."

"You all have fun. I swear, I'll just slow you down if I go with," I said.

She enveloped me into a hug and I couldn't help but notice her normal Ashley smell was masked by the cheap wine she'd been drinking. "I love you, Sister."

"Love you, too," I said.

After she and Mallory were long gone, I loosened the tie on the dress and took my hair out of its fishtail braid. I climbed up the rickety ladder, into her lofted bed, and fell asleep right as my head hit the pillow, just like I'd promised.

———

I got the full download on the Ashley-Yael situation the next morning, and they both decided that they were interested in being exclusive with each other. We scarfed down our bottomless brunch in the dining hall until I was sure someone would have to roll me out. I decided that it was time I go check on Norma to make sure she hadn't been towed yet, and for me to start the journey home.

Ashley walked me to the car, and sure enough, there were two parking tickets flapping underneath the windshield wipers. I plucked them out before turning back to Ashley and giving her one last bear hug. I thanked her again for letting me invade on her personal time and space, and reminded her to apologize to Isabel on my behalf for coming up unannounced.

"Stop," she said. "You're always welcome here."

"Has anyone ever told you that you're the greatest?" I asked.

"Are you sure you don't want me to come back with you for a few days? I can make it work with my classes. You and Mom are my number one priority."

"We'll be fine," I said. "And your number one priority right now should be you and your classes. I swear, if you come down unannounced because you're worried about me I'll be super pissed."

"Fine, I won't do it," she said. She rubbed her hand up and down my shoulder. "See, I've always been right about one thing. You're stronger than you think, Savvy. The fact that you're helping to put my school and my happiness first is a huge sign of maturity."

"If this is what adulting feels like, I'm not sure that I like it," I said.

"No one ever said adulting was easy," she replied.

"I mean, technically you just said 'adulting was easy' in your sentence," I said.

She smacked my arm. "Who invited the smart-ass?"

"You know you love it," I said.

"I do," she said. "Come here, you little weirdo. Promise me that you'll drive safe. I don't want to get any scary calls about Norma doing any NASCAR-style effects on the high-way, you hear me?"

"I'll try my best to keep her in check," I said, pulling

away from her hug. "I'll text you as soon as I get home. Promise."

"Good," she said. I stepped into the car, slamming the door behind me in a way to signify to myself that it was time to go. I could have stayed there talking to her for an eternity, but I knew I'd already overstayed my welcome. It was time to get back to my normal life and to my very cute and rambunctious white poodle.

I watched her wave in my rearview mirror until she looked like a tiny ant in the distance. It had been so comforting to see her, but it also gave me a new sense of unease about what my own college future might look like. I might not want to be at the same college as Ashley, which I always thought I would want. Maybe the two pieces of our college puzzle weren't meant to fit together like I always imagined.

chapter TWELVE

I f I was being completely honest, the only reason that I absolutely *could not* wait two days until our Monday session to hand-deliver a practice quiz to George was because I needed to see his face. And when my need to see someone's face outweighs my decision to stay in bed for the night, that person must be pretty damn cool.

A compact car that I didn't recognize sat in his driveway as I pulled into their cul-de-sac, so I opted to park on the street. According to Hannah's frequently updated Instagram story, she, at least, was home. George only made very begrudging cameos on social media, usually at the hands of Hannah. This made looking into his past life before he moved to Springdale extremely frustrating and, quite frankly, unfair. And, no matter how many times I pleaded with Grace for a single embarrassing Christmas card from George Smith Past, she refused to show me, stating that it went against "family code."

I rang the doorbell and heard someone's feet quickly shuffle to the door to meet me. Mrs. Smith greeted me on the other side, with a smile that spread across her entire face. Since we were about the same height, it was nice to get the full impact of her dazzling smile without having to strain my neck to look up. This is something that tall people never have to worry about. Looking up can be painful.

"Savannah! Come on in. George is teaching a lesson in the office. Can I get you a glass of water? A soda?" she asked.

Because George's mom is a lovely human, I bit my tongue on the soda comment. I didn't need to involve her in my passionate crusade to make *pop* the definitive term for the carbonated drink formerly known as soda.

"Oh, I don't have to stay. I just wanted to drop off a practice quiz for George. I forgot to print this one out and give it to him during our last session," I said.

"Nonsense! He'll be done in about ten minutes. Come on, let me grab you a drink," she said, leading me into the kitchen.

A sense of familiarity and comfort fell over me, coming back into this kitchen. Even though our dinner here had been only a few nights ago, I felt like I'd been welcomed into this space long before. I felt a peace here in this space that I'd lost in my own kitchen.

"I wanted to thank you again for letting me come to dinner the other night," I said.

"Of course!" Mrs. Smith said. "We were happy to have you. You were very sweet to come and watch Georgie play. I know it really meant a lot to him."

"It was seriously so cool," I said. "I mean, I knew he had to be talented, but I didn't know just *how* good he was."

Her smile multiplied times infinity.

"Have you decided on a drink?" she asked.

As much as I would love some one-on-one time with Mrs. Smith, my growing need to see George's face was too great. It suddenly became imperative to even get a little glimpse of him, and my legs bounced up and down in the anticipation of seeing him again.

"Actually, I have to use the restroom," I said.

"Sure thing! Down the hall and to the left," she said.

I started to walk down the hallway toward the bathroom but instead followed what sounded like a goose squawking. The squawking came in timed intervals, which was further proof that there wasn't, in fact, a dying goose in the next room, but a kid learning how to play an instrument, aka my own personal nightmare.

The door to the office was cracked slightly and I could see the back of George's head as he sat across from the tiniest human in pigtails. She huffed out a frustrated breath and set down the instrument that I identified as a clarinet thanks to my very scholarly exposure to the instrument from *SpongeBob* over the years.

"I'll never get it," she said.

"You're so close, Adelaide! Let's do another breathing exercise, okay?" he said. He had suddenly become so animated as he encouraged her to sit forward in her chair and take a deep breath. He counted in time as she took breaths in and out, with words of encouragement to keep her motivated along the way.

"Pretend like you're blowing out all the candles on the biggest birthday cake you've ever seen!" he said, stretching his arms out as wide as they would go.

Her eyes sparkled back up at him, and I could tell that mine were equally as sparkly. Teacher George was unlike any other type of George I'd seen up to this point, but he was quickly becoming my favorite. Well, behind Blushing George, of course.

"All right, now we're going to try it with the mouthpiece attached. Are you ready to make some music, Adelaide?" he asked.

She nodded enthusiastically, the dejected girl from a few minutes ago far gone. George attached the mouthpiece to the rest of the clarinet and held it up to Adelaide's mouth.

"Remember how we practiced your embouchure? Yep,

that's right, keep that lip from creeping up there. Good. Now, just like we were practicing before, blow with that same breath. Direct, through the instrument," he said.

Nothing but any airy sound followed by a loud squeak came out at first, and Adelaide was on the verge of pouting again.

"That's okay! You're almost there!" he said. "Tongue forward, and . . . again!"

This time a note emitted from the clarinet and it made my heart soar. Adelaide started giggling and tried a few more times to get the note out, hitting it each time after.

"You did it! Yes! That's open G, Adelaide, you played an open G!" he said. "Playing an instrument is all about perseverance. If you don't get it at first, stay positive and keep practicing until you do. Keep practicing this note and it will get a little less squeaky. Can you practice for me before we meet next week?"

"Mom said that I'm not allowed to squeak so much in the house," she said.

"Well, tell your mom that you're practicing so that it doesn't sound like squeaks anymore. Or I can recommend my favorite noise-canceling headphones for her to wear while you practice. Give me a high five. Today was awesome! Great work, Adelaide," he said.

George finally turned around to open the door to walk

Adelaide out of the office and his hand froze just above the handle when he saw me in the hallway. My heart jumped into my throat and my blood tingled as it worked its way through my body. A small half smile crept onto his face before he turned back to Adelaide.

"Adelaide, this is my friend Savannah," he said. "Can you tell her what you just accomplished today?"

"An open G!" she said with a toothy grin. "Do you play clarinet, too? Or do you play saxophone like Mr. George?"

"I wish! I can't play an instrument," I said. "My mom never forced me to play piano, and I think I might resent her a little bit for my lack of talent for the rest of my life."

"Well, he can teach you how to play. He's a good teacher," she said.

George quickly became Blushing George, and my heart continued to melt in a puddle on the floor.

"Maybe I'll have him teach me sometime," I said.

"Well, I'm going to go walk Adelaide out to her mom's car, but I'll be back in a second," he said.

He led Adelaide down the hallway before she yelled, "Good-bye, Savannah!" over her shoulder. I waved back at them until I assessed my situation.

I'd come to a guy's house, unannounced, and just crept on him while he was doing his job. If there had been any chance that he was remotely starting to like me, I probably blew it in one fell swoop by showing up here today. I had two options in this situation: sneak out the back without telling anyone, or wait for him to come back and ask (politely, because it's George) for me to leave. Before I even had the chance to be politely rejected by George, I decided to save myself from the pain. I started heading toward the sliding glass doors at the back of the office when I heard footsteps shuffling back down the hallway.

In an effort to look like I hadn't been planning a masterful escape just seconds before, I sat down in the seat where Adelaide had just left as George reappeared in the doorway.

"Savannah Alverson, as I live and breathe," he said.

"Surprise?" I said, my voice going up an octave at the end of the word.

"What brings you to my practice room today?" he asked, sinking into the chair across from me.

"I heard you're especially good at teaching people how to play open G on the clarinet. Coincidentally, it's my dying wish to learn how to play," I said.

"You're dying?" he asked, raising his eyebrows.

"We're all dying, George. We're all part of this big wheel called life," I said.

"Hmm, yes, I've heard of this wheel before," he said. "Well, you're in luck that I happen to have a clarinet on hand courtesy of Hannah's brief stint with playing. I can't promise that it's the cleanest instrument ever, but it still works."

"That's what counts," I said. "As long as I can fulfill my dying wish of the open G."

He audibly snickered, and the butterflies in my stomach had a celebratory dance party. I could spend a whole lifetime just trying to make George laugh.

"So are you serious? Do you really want to learn?" he asked.

"I'm always serious," I said.

He shook his head and hesitated for a few moments before opening up the old clarinet case and reaching inside, pulling out the mouthpiece and taking off parts that I had no idea of their purpose. He put a small piece of wood under his tongue for a few seconds before attaching it to the mouthpiece. I watched him place just the mouthpiece in his mouth before he blew into it, making arguably the worst noise in human history.

"What was that for?" I asked.

"This is how you start to learn! You have to work up to Adelaide's level," he said.

He handed the mouthpiece over to me and went into a detailed description of how to properly adjust your lips around the mouthpiece and how your tongue should hit the reed, and all this talk of mouths and tongues in the presence of George did nothing for my concentration. I mostly nodded and smiled as I watched his lips move and imagined other, very PG-13 scenarios involving George's lips.

A deafening squeak erupted from the mouthpiece when I blew into it for the first time and I wished, for both of our sakes, that I would have had a few more seconds to sneak out the sliding glass doors. We were both trapped in this situation that neither of us wanted to be in because I had to play it cool.

"On a positive note, I think you might have broken my record for loudest first attempt ever," he said.

"I don't realize my own strength sometimes. R.I.P. to your eardrums and all eardrums within a mile radius," I said.

"Let's do that again, but this time . . . less force," he said.

This time it was less of a squeak and more of an obnoxious buzz, which I took as a good sign. He pulled out the clarinet case again and started to assemble the rest of it.

"So, how often do you teach lessons?" I asked.

"Right now I have three kids who come in for lessons. Most of the young ones come in for clarinet because they usually teach clarinet first before you can switch to saxophone. It's just a little something to make some extra money here and there. Plus, it's good practice, since I want to be a music teacher down the road," he said.

He handed me the rest of the clarinet, and I attached the

mouthpiece. I let it sit in my lap for a few seconds, and I almost felt like a real player. Almost, until I remembered the first horrific sound that I produced.

Just before more nervous words tumbled out of my mouth, George scooted closer to me, rendering me speechless (which is very difficult to do, mind you). He picked up the clarinet from my lap and held it out in front of him.

"You see how your thumb rests here? This is how you hold it," he said.

I took it back from him and placed it on my thumb. He raised his eyebrows to me, asking silently if he could adjust its position in my hands, and I nodded. His fingers grazed mine as he repositioned the instrument on my thumb, and I wondered if he could feel the same spark that went through my fingertips in that moment.

"So open G is just blowing the same amount of air as before, but through the instrument. Easy enough, right?" he asked.

"For most people, yes, but I'll mess it up somehow," I said.

"Impossible," he said, "Not when I'm right here. Make sure that you're tilted down a bit—yep, just like that."

This time a more refined sound came out around us and for the first time in my life, I was making actual music. Sure, my benchmark had been an eight-year-old completing the same task in less time and with better sound, but I still did it. George really must be a miracle worker of a teacher.

"I did it!"

"Is Savannah Alverson genuinely shocked about something? I never thought that I'd see the day," he said.

"There seems to be a lot of that going down with you around," I said.

"Is that a bad thing?" he asked, raising his eyebrows. I was suddenly very aware of how close we were sitting, our knees nearly touching and his arm braced against the back of my chair.

"Definitely not a bad thing," I said.

The space around us snapped and crackled with energy, and it felt like we were most definitely in the middle of a *moment*. A moment that could only last so long in my unlucky universe.

"There you are!" Mrs. Smith said at the doorway. "I was worried about you when you didn't come back after a while. But I see you found George!"

"Yep, we're doing great, Mom, thanks," Blushing George said.

"Savannah, would you like to stay for dinner?" Mrs. Smith asked.

"Um, thank you so much for the offer, but I'm meeting Grace tonight to talk about a school project," I said.

"Next time! You're welcome anytime, dear!" she said.

"Thank you so much," I said, smiling. George sat silently in the chair next to me. I tried to look back over at him, but he refused to make eye contact with me. Mrs. Smith left, and George started to pull the clarinet back apart to put away.

"So . . . I guess I'll see you at school Monday?" I said.

"I guess," he said, still not meeting my gaze.

"Thanks for the lesson. What do I owe you? I can pay in pizza or rap performances. Up to you," I said.

"Ah, I'll send a bill your way," he said, barely playing along.

"Okay, see you tomorrow," I said.

"See you," he replied, closing the case and standing up to put it away. I waited around for a few beats to see if he'd turn around, but he continued to unnecessarily rearrange things in the closet across the room. I turned and left, secretly hoping that he would call back out to me and we could pick up our banter right where we left it, but he didn't.

They should put a warning on all clarinet cases: May Cause Sexual Tension.

chapter THIRTEEN

When I regathered my composure the next morning after the Clarinet Incident, I decided to write it off as a very one-sided admiration. This wasn't my first rodeo in Unrequited Land. In fact, I had a season pass. Each new crush, I'd find myself standing there, fast pass in hand, wishing that someone who had zero interest in me would finally open their eyes and see me standing in front of them.

Talking about Unrequited Land with Ashley or Grace was always a dead end because neither of them ever visited. They'd never had a problem finding someone who was interested in them—in fact, once they would break things off with someone they were dating, someone new would come in line and express interest. It was like they sent out a beacon that screamed "I'm incredibly datable," and I sent out a beacon that screamed, "Look at the two other options right next to me."

So, there I sat once again, in the front seat of a new

friend-zone roller coaster that I wasn't sure my heart was prepared to handle. This one stung more than others, for some reason. Possibly because this was the first time I actually believed that George was my ticket to the emotional and physical theme park that everyone around me had been able to go to for years. Maybe I was just one of those people meant to ride the roller coaster to the top, peek over at everyone else across the way, but never actually join them.

Fiyero and I snuggled up on the couch, watching an incredibly informative documentary on Lady Gaga, with two slices of peanut butter–banana toast. I snuck Fiyero small chunks of banana with a little bit of peanut butter coating the outside. And I used to tease Ashley that she spoiled him. Geesh, I'd become a softie.

It was still early enough on a Sunday morning that I thought I was in the clear from a Mom drop-in for the next few hours. She worked ridiculous hours at her PR firm, always agreeing to work later than necessary to "make up" for the time she took off to be on *Shake the Weight*. When she first got back from *Shake the Weight*, she made the grand declaration that she would use her connections and influence to be an Internet celebrity, vowing never to step back into the "hellhole" that she'd dedicated so many years of her life to. But, after two considerable Instagram sponsorships fell through, Mom had to approach her old boss with her tail between her legs, selling a little piece of her soul on the dotted line.

I wasn't sure what our interaction would be like when she woke up, anyway. We were still on rocky terms after I confronted her when I got home from George's last week, and we'd barely spoken since. This wasn't entirely new for us. We went through our rounds of fights throughout the years with long periods of silence, but it felt more severe without having Ashley here to add more noise back into the house.

"Fiyero?" I asked. He cocked his head to the side, suddenly alert. "Do you . . . want to go outside?"

He dashed from one end of the living room to the other in his excitement, and I giggled, leading him to the back door. He barreled out into the backyard the second the door opened, grabbing for his favorite blue-and-yellow rope toy to play fetch with. I fought with him to get him to drop the toy, and once I did, he would dash across the yard in preparation for me to throw to him. We played like this for over a half an hour, until my arm felt like it would actually fall off from Fiyero tugging on it so hard. I sank to the ground and let him come over and cover my face in slobbery kisses, knocking me to my back. In these moments, he still believed he was a puppy, but I was intensely aware that he was a fifty-pound poodle monster.

"Oof, I can't breathe, buddy!" I exclaimed, well, barely managed to vocalize.

The back door opened and he ran to greet the new person who was awake.

"Hey, Mom," I said.

"Good morning, Savvy," she said. She kissed Fiyero on the head before wrapping her robe tighter around her. "It's a little chilly."

"Not terrible for October," I said. Indiana had the most unpredictable weather. One day it could be a sweltering ninety-five degrees, and the next it could drop to a brisk fifty degrees without anyone batting an eye.

"Why don't you come inside?" she asked.

"Sure," I said, rolling over to hoist myself back up after the attack of the poodle monster. I brushed the grass off that covered my butt and I imagined her watching with radar eyes, zoning in on the fat on my thighs and backside jiggling. I suddenly wished that I had a robe to pull over myself, too.

I wondered if this would be the moment where she defended all her actions and I would apologize to make peace, like always. I wondered if she thought about anything I'd said, or took any of it to heart. I hoped so.

She poured herself a cup of coffee with a touch of vanilla creamer, her one indulgence that she couldn't seem to shake, and took up her post at the head of the table. I joined her tentatively, still unsure about what move to make in our delicate dance.

"Did you already eat?" she asked.

"Yep," I replied, hoping she wouldn't push further.

"What did you have?"

Here we go.

"Peanut butter toast," I said.

She cringed ever so slightly but didn't actually say anything. I wonder if Ashley had talked to her lately. Mom always held back when she got a good guilt trip from Ashley.

"Talked to Ashley lately?" I asked.

"Last night," she said, taking a long sip of coffee. "She's going to start working on a student film with an upperclassman. Did she tell you all about that?"

No. "Yeah, she told me about that a while ago."

"And how was this Yael girl? Did you see her when you visited her? Is she a good influence on your sister?" she asked.

"I think she makes her happy," I said. "I didn't actually hang out much with them. It was a lot of Savvy-Ashley time."

"Good. I'm glad you girls got to spend some time together," she said. She ran her hand through her hair and looked at the clock on our newly installed gas stove. It looked fancy and out of place in our dated kitchen, but Mom's health coach swore by the benefits of cooking on a gas range, so one was installed right after she left the show.

"What are you doing today?" she asked.

Shocked, I snapped my head back to make direct eye contact with her.

"Nothing really. Why?" I asked.

"Maybe we need some Savvy-Mom time. We could go see that new Zac Efron movie, or go mini-golfing, or go get our nails done like we used to when I'd call you girls out early from school on those Fridays. What do you say?" she asked.

Some of my favorite memories came from those days where Mom let us ditch school for a few hours to hang out with her. I remember signing out of school the last Friday of every month for all of middle school, for "appointments" Mom would write us loose for. The secretary had to think that we had perpetual cavities forming in our mouths the amount of times we went to the dentist those years.

"Sure," I said. It still seemed too good to be true, like someone had taken up residence in my mom and made her an agreeable person all of a sudden. It was very unnerving. But it sparked a little bit of hope inside my chest that I hadn't felt in a really long time.

"I'll look up some movie times, then we can grab lunch and maybe shop around the mall afterward? How does that sound?" she asked.

"It sounds great," I said, smiling. It sounded like the best plan we'd had in quite some time. "I'll go get dressed."

I went back and forth between wearing one of my favorite A-line dresses with bright pink and orange flowers, or going the more comfortable route of jeans and a T-shirt. Then I thought about my hindered ability to sprawl out in the movie theater seat with the dress option and firmly landed on the comfy side of things. Zac Efron would have to accept me for my casual comfort.

When I came back downstairs, Mom was wearing one of her old green dresses that she always used to wear, but this time, with a belt around the waist to define it. I hadn't seen her pull out anything from her old wardrobe since she came back from the show, and a part of me wondered if she'd ritualistically burned them in an effort to erase her past self.

"I love that dress," I said. She turned around, tugging on the stretchy fabric.

"It does nothing for my figure," she said, pulling at the belt tighter.

"But it makes your eyes pop! You seriously look gorgeous," I said.

"Well, hopefully you won't see me in this again. I need to drop another fifteen pounds to fit back into my regular clothes," she said, a shaking hand running through her hair.

That same, angry fire that lit my belly a week ago sparked again, and I thought I might explode all over the room in a fireball of anger. Here she was, looking actually *healthy* again for the first time in a long time, and wearing one of my favorite dresses that felt like home and normalcy to me, and she wanted to devalue it. To devalue herself.

"But these are your regular clothes," I said. "That's the dress you wore to my middle school graduation, and the one you wore to Ashley's first film screening. You used to be beautiful in it."

"I never felt beautiful in this dress," she snapped.

"You were beautiful to me in this dress," I said.

She was silent for a few moments before grabbing her keys near the front door.

"Are you ready to go?" she asked, not looking back to see if I followed her out the door. I hastily locked up behind her before sliding into the front seat of our family SUV.

This car had never been Mom's choice. If it would have been up to Mom, we would have gotten a practical minivan or a compact family car that took up less gas—or less space in general. But Dad refused to let his family image ruin his car reputation. So he got us the biggest, flashiest, black SUV that the dealership had available. It used to be his project to get the car detailed and washed once a week, but ever since he left, the SUV had been collecting dirt and scratches without much of a care in the world. I wondered, sometimes, why Mom had kept it for all this time.

We pulled into the familiar parking lot of the Springdale Mall, which was packed with the weekend crowd getting in to see a movie before the matinee was up. We parked farther out than probably was necessary, but Mom always complained about maneuvering in between smaller cars in our beast. I could hardly blame her, since I could barely park Norma the Nissan properly, let alone a honking SUV.

My phone buzzed in my pocket as we parked and my heart flip-flopped. There was a 99.9 percent chance that this was just my phone service provider letting me know that my data plan was almost up for the month after I binged a whole season of *Project Runway* on my tablet without being connected to WiFi. (Honestly, imagine my horror when I realized that I hadn't been connected all day.) But the .01 percent chance of this text being from George made my hands shake.

George: A student of mine had to reschedule a lesson for Monday night, so I can't study. Sorry for the late notice.

Have you ever had all your fears confirmed so fully in one sentence? I stared at the text for a few moments before putting my phone back in my pocket. I'd thoroughly freaked him out, and now his precalc grade could be in jeopardy. What would Mr. Kavach say if he knew I was personally responsible for bringing George's grade down that week because of my clarinet-induced flirtation?

"Everything okay?" Mom asked, hand resting on the door.

"Peachy!" I said, promptly getting out of the car. Anything to avoid talking about George with my mom. "Let's go enjoy some Zac Efron man candy."

"Why do you have to say it like that?" she asked, a tiny smile creeping onto her face. The first smile that I'd seen from her in what felt like a million years.

"Because we're not paying ten dollars apiece to learn about the innerworkings of fraternity life. We're here to look unabashedly at Mr. Efron for two hours," I said.

She shook her head, her smile growing bigger. "Oh, Savannah Lynn."

We'd almost made it to the door when I heard the typical pitch of someone who had just realized they were going to have to stop and say hello to my mom and probably occupy the next ten minutes of our lives with her chitchat. Our old neighbor, Lois Goodman.

"Kim, is that you?" Lois's voice screeched from behind us.

Mom stopped dead in her tracks as she forced a smile onto her face before turning toward the always-overly-enthusiastic Lois Goodman.

"Lois! How nice to see you!" she said.

"Well, look at you! Don't you look wonderful!" she said, motioning for Mom to twirl around. She did so, reluctantly, and I noticed the faintest redness creeping up on her neck and to her face.

"Oh, I watched every episode of the show," Lois Goodman said. "I can't believe you just lost to that Dave guy. It's unfair. It's a known fact that guys lose weight faster than girls. You'd think they'd consider that by now!"

"I wasn't on there to win," Mom said. "I just wanted help making a life change."

"How has it been keeping up? Do you have a personal trainer here? Are you thinking of becoming one to help people out who were in your situation?" she asked.

I could sense Mom retreating within herself. I'd watched her struggle with the fact that with work, she hadn't been able to keep the weight off like she thought she could. Because what they were pushing her through on the show, the constant, relentless training that no body is meant to endure, it wasn't a realistic change. Losing weight that quickly was like pushing a ball underwater, but bodies can't keep the ball under forever. It will eventually spring back up to its natural, stable weight. And I didn't know if Mom would ever be ready for her ball to shoot back up from her slipping grasp.

"I'm working out on my own. I have a plan that I developed with my trainer on the show, and I'm keeping up with it," she said.

Lois Goodman reached out and touched Mom's arm, and Mom took one step backward. Lois didn't seem to notice.

"Well, I'm proud of you for all your hard work. I can't imagine the payoff. And to be single in this new body? You must be having so much fun dating! I'm quite jealous," she said, giggling.

Mom's face sunk in even further. She gave Lois Goodman a tight smile before linking her arm through mine, a very uncharacteristic move.

"Well, Savannah and I have a movie to go catch. It was great to chat with you, Lois," Mom said.

"So lovely, dear! I'd love to chat with you sometime about your workout regimen. I know Cal wants to get us on a solid plan for the New Year. I'll call you!" she said.

"Sounds good," Mom said, raising her hand in a final wave before turning us toward the mall.

We got our tickets and sat in the movie theater next to each other for the next two hours without speaking. Not even an effortlessly charming Zac Efron could keep Mom's attention. She sat through the whole movie in an entirely different world, her eyes glazing over and having no physical reactions to the movie (even when Zac Efron surprised the love interest at the end with a dramatic, romantic gesture that ended in a steamy kiss).

As the credits rolled, I stood up, and she seemed to shake out of whatever state she fell into during the movie. She picked up her purse from in between her feet and started her descent down the stairs.

"So, what did you think of the ending?" I asked.

"Huh?" she asked.

"The ending. Did you like how the movie ended?" I asked.

"Oh, yeah, sure," she said. She started to pick up her pace out of the movie theater, and I had to seriously power walk to catch up to her.

"Uh, where to next?" I asked. "Lunch? Nails? Shopping? All of the above?"

"Actually, I just remembered that I need to do something for work. I'm so sorry, Savvy. I think we need to go home," she said.

All the happiness and hopefulness came crashing down

inside of me. Each piece of normalcy and love that Mom had thrown my way today built onto one another like Jenga blocks, and she'd just pulled out the weakest piece, causing it all to crumble in on itself.

I nodded. All was back to New Normal.

chapter FOURTEEN

"**H**ave I told you lately how thankful I am that your boy-friend happens to be athletically inclined?" I asked as Grace and I walked into Springdale High School the follow-ing Thursday after school. There was something eerie about walking through the halls without that familiar, if not annoying, faces of your classmates surrounding you. It made me miss the hubbub. Only a little.

Ben had been kind enough to lend us his student-athlete pass to access the gymnasium outside of school hours, and we were about to witness firsthand the battle royal that would go down between the dance team and the base-ball team, who each felt like they deserved the room for practice.

We had it on good word from Melinda Aldridge that they were especially fed up by the baseball team's latest antics, and they were ready to reclaim their rightful practice spot in the gymnasium, especially with the homecoming game quickly approaching and with no other logical place to practice.

Although the practice wasn't *technically* open, we'd had verbal confirmation from Melinda that we could observe the dance team rehearsal. And if we *happened* to walk into the baseball team's practice, it would be a total coincidence that we never could have predicted happening.

We peeked into the window of the gymnasium, and, in our heads, we both planned out our sneakiest strategy of getting in there unnoticed. We just had to wait for the perfect moment to enter the gym when no one would notice us.

"While we're here," Grace whispered. "My mom is making reservations for homecoming. She said Luigi's gets booked really early."

"That's good thinking on Mrs. M's part," I said.

"You'll bring George, right?" Grace asked.

"Ah, I'm actually not sure that he'd be up for it," I said.

"What! No way! Did something happen? Did you not tell me something?" she hissed. Her whispering was basically yelling at this point. The whole school could understand now that George and I had an awkward moment and I was now firmly a visitor in Unrequited Land.

"Um, we're on official paper business right now," I said.

"Why aren't you taking George to homecoming?" Grace asked, steamrolling over my request for professionalism.

"Because he hasn't asked me? Because he canceled our study session on Monday in the most obvious sign of 'I'm not interested' in the world?" I said.

"He's new to school! He doesn't know when it is. Plus, he's shy. You're, like, the complete opposite of shy. Help him out! Ask him! He'll say yes!" she said.

I shook my head. "He doesn't like me. I saw the Look, where he wanted me to get out of his general area and leave forever because the thought of having to kiss me absolutely repulsed him."

"I think you're being a tad dramatic," she said, putting her hands on her hips. "I've seen you two together. He likes you."

"Boys don't *like* like me, Grace. It's just a fact that I've grown to accept," I said.

"Bullshit!" Grace said. She shouted it so loud that she shrunk a little bit as it echoed down the hallway. We really weren't keeping our position secret anymore. "You're the queen of pushing people away before they can say they like you. The *queen* of rejecting first so you can't be rejected."

"That's not true. Not one person has ever asked me out before," I said.

"Because you don't give them a chance! You shut them

down, talk about being great friends, and even talk about how you're going to be alone forever in front of them. That's not really an open invitation to ask someone out, is it?" she asked.

"If I looked like you, they might still try," I said.

The hallway was quiet for a few beats before she finally replied.

"What are you talking about?" she asked.

"I'm fine with how I look. And trust me, I'm not going to ever support making drastic changes to a body, like my mom, to get attention from people, but it's just never *easy*. The minute you break up with someone, you have a whole line of guys waiting to take you out on a date. You have to realize that, right?" I said.

"It's not about how I look, Savvy, it's about how I treat people. It's about how I'm open to letting new people into my life," she said.

I shook my head, feeling my anger starting to boil behind my ears, turning my whole head hot with fury. If we stayed here any longer, tears would start to spring out of my eyes. And there's no crying in baseball practice.

"I let new people in. That's not the problem," I said.

"Isn't it?" she asked. "Coming from the girl who pushed Saint George away for the first few weeks of knowing him because it scared her how easily they clicked right away?"

As much as it pained me to admit, she had the tiniest bit of a point. I *had* pushed George away so hard at the beginning of our friendship for that reason. I didn't click with people like that. And, to be honest, it scared me.

"Maybe you're right," I said.

"You can be a little intimidating sometimes," she said.

I scoffed. "You've got to be kidding."

"I'm not! You're so smart, and quick on your feet, and have this 'Savvy against the world' attitude that makes it hard for *me* to even feel like I know the right thing to say back to you sometimes. I guess . . . I wish you believed in yourself in the same way you project yourself to the world, because you're fierce, funny, and hella loyal. There's no one on this planet that I'd rather have in my corner," she said.

"Just this planet?" I teased.

She pushed my shoulder, laughing. "See? That."

"You think I've scared him off?" I asked.

"No way," she said. "But I *do* think he is of a rarer, quieter breed. A breed that doesn't always make the first move. So ask him out, ask him about the dance, and I'm sure he'll say yes."

"You're sure?" I asked.

"A good friend doesn't lie. And I hope you think I'm a good friend," she said, leaning into my shoulder.

"I do," I said, taking her hand in mine. We sat there for

a while, taking in the musky smell of the boys' locker room on the other side of the hallway. It was a distinct smell that my nostrils would never be able to forget, and would perpetually associate with the hideous Coach Triad. That whole interview with him still made me shudder.

"Time to do some super sleuthing?" she asked. She stood up and held a hand out to me to help me up from the ground.

"Indeed," I said, taking it and letting her pull me the rest of the way up.

We figured that our best bet would be to get into the girls' locker room and shuffle our way to the emergency ladder at the corner of the gym. From there we'd perch up at the top of the bleachers, where we had the potential to be hidden behind the electronic scoreboard.

Halfway up the incredibly steep ladder to get to the top of the bleachers, I regretted this decision so hard. Heights and I were not friends, and if I looked down now, I felt like I might vomit all over the squeaky-clean gymnasium floor. Good thing Grace went first. At least she wouldn't have to experience the vom.

"Are we almost there?" I asked, my vision starting to go spotty. If we didn't make it up this ladder in a reasonable amount of time, I was going to go *splat* on the floor, and we would most definitely be caught for spying on Triad.

"Three more rungs!" Grace whispered down to me. I had to keep my eyes firmly closed for two reasons: the impending doom that lay below, and the fact that Grace had chosen to wear a miniskirt that day.

When I finally felt flat ground, I sprawled onto it while Grace pulled me the rest of the way onto the bleacher. Thankfully, the team was practicing running drills up and down the gym, so no one could hear my body scraping across the bleacher as Grace maneuvered me.

"Are you doing okay?" she whispered.

I managed to give her a thumbs-up with a small moan. She took this as her cue to take notes and be attentive while I collected myself.

"Melinda said they would be here by now," Grace whispered.

For the next five minutes, all we heard was Coach Triad yelling at people to run harder and pick up the pace, and I figured that this was my own hell. Being at the very top of the bleachers while listening to a misogynistic coach yell at people while he sat on his ass. Confirmed. Grace and I were in Savannah's Personal Hell.

"Oh, crap, I think someone spotted me," she said.

She ducked down, and I felt like I could be one with the gymnasium again. I took my turn to pop my head up and observe. I heard a door open underneath us, and Melinda and the rest of the dance team walked out of the girls' locker room.

"Showtime!" I said, smacking Grace's leg.

Jolene Foster, the dance team coach, came up to Triad and handed him a sheet of paper. He looked at it for a few seconds before handing it back to her and actually *shooing* her away. She pointed again to the paper, and I wished that the baseball guys would stop running so we could hear their exchange.

"We've got to get down there," I said. "We have to know what she's saying."

I started to make my way toward the ladder before Grace had a chance to stop me. We had to hear what was going on.

"Savvy!" she hissed at me.

About halfway down I felt those same stars begin to dot my vision and the overwhelming nausea take over again. I knew that I had to get down the rest of this ladder, fast, before something bad happened.

Everything around me suddenly sounded like it was muffled underwater. I could hear Grace calling out my name as I completely lost my vision, and I could hear Coach Triad bounding up to us and yelling profanities as he discovered that we'd snuck in. The last thing that I heard was a high-pitched "Savannah!" before everything went dark.

". . . you had no right coming into my practice unannounced. I would have given you permission to observe with an official press pass through the principal if you would have asked. Don't think this is going to be brushed under the rug," I could hear Triad saying.

My eyes refused to open, the darkness still surrounding me.

"We're so sorry, sir," I heard Grace saying. "We had a firm belief that we wouldn't be observing a typical practice environment if we came with your knowledge, and we wanted to have the most authentic take on the baseball experience at Springdale as possible."

I could practically hear her eyelashes batting at him. For her, it might just work.

"So how do you explain this?" he asked. "Is this supposed to be me?"

"Uh—" Grace started.

My eyes sprang open and I turned to see Coach Triad, Jolene Foster, and Grace hovering over me.

"I'm more of a caricature artist. I exaggerate certain features," I said.

Everyone's eyes snapped to me. Grace knelt down beside me and wrapped me in a hug, helping me to sit up. Every part of my body hurt, and I was convinced that I had become a giant, human bruise. I winced as she let me go and laid me back down.

"Why didn't you let me go first! Oh my God, this could have been so much worse!" she said.

Coach Triad was still holding up my page of notes, where I'd drawn a very true-to-life depiction of him with his face in a super frown. Jolene Foster looked like she was trying to hold back a laugh when she looked at the notes as she turned back to face me.

"Those are private notes," I said.

"Private my ass," Triad said. "If I see either of you sniffing around practice again, I'm going to have to make a formal complaint to the principal."

"Yes, sir, of course, sir," Grace said. She lifted me up off the floor and, while the world spun for a few moments, I was able to carry myself out of the gym without a problem.

"Oh my God, Savvy, are you all right?" Grace asked as we left.

"I only fell down a few rungs, it's no big deal," I said.

"You passed out!" she said.

"For, like, point two seconds. I could hear every bad-mouthing thing that Triad said," I said.

"Should I call your mom? Should I take you to the doctor?" she asked.

"Really, I'm fine," I said. "I swear, I only passed out because my body realized how far off the ground I was. The only damage will probably be my butt, since I landed there first. I can already feel an epic bruise coming on."

"If you're sure . . . ," she said.

"I'm sure," I said. "Besides, we got great notes for the story. That's what we came for, right?"

She dropped me off at my house, and I found one of those neck pillows that you get at the airport, to sit on. Even sitting on my cozy couch was painful. I couldn't even imagine going to school and sitting on the hard seats for eight hours the next day.

As I went back over my notes from the day, my phone buzzed in my pocket.

Grace: I texted Melinda for details after we left. Apparently Ms. Foster got a petition signed by school officials to grant the dance team the gymnasium until the homecoming game. Those were the papers that she showed him. Triad refused to leave, and Principal Laurence had to come down and ask him to move his practice outside. Wild!

Me: SO wild! Thanks for getting the scoop.

Grace: Of course! Take it easy, my clumsy partner in crime.

chapter FIFTEEN

My prediction of having a most painful sitting experience throughout the day had come true, and it was only first period. I couldn't image an entire rest of the day with this pain. If it was more socially acceptable to view calc class from a standing position, I would have been a much happier camper for that hour.

I couldn't stand up fast enough when the bell rang. The sweet relief of taking pressure off my backside was enough to make happy tears sting my eyes. Grace sidled up next to me as we merged out into the student traffic in the hallway.

"So, I have a proposition for you," she said.

"Nothing good ever starts with your propositions," I said.

She glowered at me. "I'm going to let that one slide since you're injured. *Anyway*, Ben is planning on having a party at his house tonight. Nothing too wild, but a chance to blow off a little steam after the game. I think you should invite George."

I started to object, but she held up her hand.

"You obviously have some tension going on there that neither of you is willing to admit right now, but with the right atmosphere, things could just be . . . easier," she said.

"Easier?" I asked.

"Parties are made for admitting your crushes. Plus, I'll be there the whole time to back you up. It's foolproof," she said.

"I don't know—"

"George!" she yelled, waving to a very startled George from down the hallway. I became super aware of the distance between George and me, and as he got closer, my body responded accordingly. I was trying to remember everything Grace had told me about intentionally pushing people away before they had the chance to reject me. I had maybe possibly jumped to the wrong conclusion during the Clarinet Incident, and I was going to try my best to go back into my ideas of more-than-friendship with George without the fear of rejection.

"Hey," he said, his eyes sliding to meet mine. His half smile absolutely killed me, the way his dimple formed just on top of it . . . the feeling of needing his face on mine was coming back in full force.

"Hi," I said, trying to sound like I wasn't imagining what his lips felt like in a very dramatic fantasy going on in my head.

"You know what? Ben mentioned that there was a party going on at his house tonight. You two should come!" she said.

I tilted my head, and she smiled at me, waggling her eyebrows. My eyes widened, begging her to stop. But George had seen it. He was officially blushing.

"Uh, sure, maybe!" I said. I wanted to die that Grace was being so obvious. Maybe George really wasn't as on the same page as I had hoped.

"I'll go if you go," he said, looking at me. "Both of you—I mean I don't know that many people."

"Yeah, we'll be there!" Grace said. The warning bell rang and she pulled me off with her. She yelled a quick "I'll text you with the address!" over her shoulder, and I followed along in a daze.

"You're trouble, Grace Moreno. I'm serious," I said. I would never admit to her the thrill that went down my spine thinking about hanging out with George in a party setting. Maybe this would be the moment that I could finally give into my overwhelming desire to kiss him.

I couldn't pay attention to anything the rest of the

day—my brain was already in party-preparation mode. What would I wear? How was I getting there? Would I have to drink to fit in? Would I like it? All of these questions bounced around like loose Ping-Pong balls in my brain and made me feel dizzy and overwhelmed.

I landed on a floral print dress that made me look tanner than I actually was. It cut right under my boobs and pushed them up to make them more pronounced. I'd never actually had a venue to wear the dress out, but I figured it would get the job done. My hair was a complete disaster and being entirely uncooperative, so I pulled it into a messy braid that came down to my right side. Little loose ends of hair jutted out here and there within the braid, but it looked pretty decent for a girl who'd learned to fishtail her own hair from a YouTube tutorial.

My phone buzzed angrily on my bathroom counter. I picked it up and found five texts from Grace saying that she was outside.

The last text read:

Grace: Get down here or I'm going to call George and tell him how badly you want to see him at this party.

That got my still-bruised butt moving. I put the last touch of bubble gum lip gloss on that I'd had since I was in middle school, and surprisingly it still looked decent (even if it was a little bit clumpy). I ran downstairs and saw Grace, phone in hand, waving to me from the front seat of her car.

"You better not have called him," I said when I opened the door.

"Of course not," she said. "But I knew it would make you get here quicker if I threatened to. By the way, you look hot."

"The hair isn't too much?" I asked.

"Absolutely not," she said, touching my carefully crafted fishtail braid. It had only taken me five tries. I think I accounted for one thousand of the views on the tutorial video I watched. "If my hair was long enough to do this, I would do it all the time."

"And the dress? Is it too much?" I asked.

"You look great, babe. Stop all this worrying and let yourself have some fun," she said.

Easier said than done, Gracie. "And Ben is okay with us crashing his party with ulterior motives?"

"More than okay," she said. "He likes to invite a bunch of different groups of people from school to his parties, not just the football team. Plus, I let him in on my secret plan, and he's all for setting you and George up."

"Oh, great," I said.

"Isn't it?" she said, ignoring my sarcasm. "The universe obviously wants you and George to be a thing."

We pulled up to Ben's house within a few minutes, and there was already a line of cars dotting the street. Apparently, Grace got driveway priority as the girlfriend of the host, so we were able to hop out of the car and into the party quickly.

Ben's house reminded me of mine—every house in our town was developed by the same builder, to be fair—but bigger. It also looked like his parents had done renovations so that the wood floor was different than the one built into the house originally, along with the beige-painted walls. There were kids taking shots in the office, and a couple making out on the stairs who we almost fell on top of as people pushed in the front door behind us. So this was the kind of party it was going to be. I hadn't mentally prepared myself enough for this.

"I'm going to go find Ben," she said. "Want to come with me?"

"Sure!" I said. Anything to get away from the massive amounts of alcohol.

We wove through our classmates who stood in their normal, cliquey groups. It seemed like everyone was pretty well represented—the athletes, drama kids, debate team—they were all here, but only speaking to those who orbited in their same social circle. I guess the newspaper kids were one circle removed from being invited to parties.

Before we could find Ben, my eyes locked on an extremely tall strawberry blond guy in the corner of the room. He was on his phone, not daring to look up. My heart leaped into my throat when I realized that he did, in fact, come. When he looked up and saw me, the smile that followed turned my insides into goop.

"Hey, you go on and find Ben. I'm going to talk to George," I said, motioning toward her cousin. He waved at both of us, and I smiled. I suddenly wished we weren't surrounded by all our classmates who were gauging everyone else's interactions. I felt their eyes on me, not only because I never came to parties, but because I was interacting with the super-cute new guy. I didn't want to be the gossip at school on Monday.

He met me in the middle of the living room, and we hung in that awkward should-we-hug-or-not limbo again. I ended up going in for the hug, knowing that I'd kick myself later if I didn't. When I pulled back I looked around us to see if people were watching. To my surprise, no one could care less. They were wrapped up in their own conversations, and no one was balking at the fact that Savannah Alverson just hugged a boy.

"I'm glad you came," I said. I could feel my blush creeping up on my face and decided I needed to justify my statement in a way that was less *Oh my God, I want to kiss your face.*

"Otherwise I would have had to sit in the corner all night while Grace and Ben made out."

"That would have been uncomfortable," he said.

"Totally," I said. My brain was fishing for any way to change the conversation, any way to *start* a conversation at least, but just being in his presence after we'd left things on Saturday was filled with so much tension.

"Did you want a drink or anything?" I asked.

"I'm good," he said. Phew. Relief. "How about you?"

"I'm good, too," I said.

"Do you want to sit down?" he asked, motioning toward the couch. The same couch where two kids from my AP lit class were currently on top of each other in a way that could not be comfortable or enjoyable. Was this my invitation to make out with him? How did this kind of thing work? I should have asked Grace for more details before the party started.

"Sure," I said. I tugged at the bottom of my braid, making sure that it was out of the way in case of potential lip-locking. I crossed my leg toward him, our legs almost touching. I could feel electricity striking between us, which made me even more self-conscious. Did he feel it, too?

"Guess who got an A on their polynomial functions quiz?" he asked.

"Really?" I said, giving him a high five. "Even though we didn't actually study on Monday? That's epic."

"I have this really cool tutor who taught me some new studying techniques so that I can practice on my own now," he said.

"Oh no, have you been seeing another tutor behind my back?" I said.

"Shut up." He laughed. He pushed my leg lightly, letting his hand linger for a few beats before sliding it back into his lap. My leg burned where he touched it. We stared at each other for a few more moments, and I felt the oh-my-God-I-want-to-kiss-your-face sensation again, but on steroids. My body started leaning toward him involuntarily. I closed my eyes, letting whatever was going to happen next, happen.

And then, I gasped out in pain, which made George's eyes shoot open and meet mine.

"Did I do something wrong?" he asked.

I put my head into my hands, not wanting to admit that the subtle shift to kiss George had sent a shooting pain up my bruised backside that made stars form in my vision.

"Not at all," I groaned. "I fell off a ladder yesterday when I was doing research for my story with Grace and hurt my . . . butt."

He held back a laugh. "You hurt your butt?"

"Like, really badly," I said.

"How come you didn't tell me you got hurt?" he asked.

"Because it was embarrassing!" I said. "I want to permanently erase the memories of that whole day forever."

"I could have—I don't know I could have, like, brought you some baked goods or something," he said.

"Brought me some baked goods?" I pressed.

"I don't know, it just would have been nice to know that you were hurt!"

I smiled, realizing in that moment that maybe Grace had been a little right. That maybe George cared about my well-being as more than just a friend, and we were both actually on the same page. I let my knee fall to touch his, and just the pressure of our knees touching was enough to make my entire body sparkle with anticipation.

"I'm sorry," I said. "I should have told you."

"It's okay," he said, staring at me for a few seconds too long. This had to be it. This had to be the moment that we'd both held back on out of politeness or fear. George and I were about to kiss, and every part of me ached for him to just reach out already and—

"I actually could use a drink," he said, standing up abruptly. He was halfway to the kitchen before I could even respond.

I sat there, blinking in the wake of another George rejection, wondering how I could keep being so wrong about all the signals I thought I was picking up on. Maybe this whole time I'd been exaggerating what this could be. Maybe he just thought of me as a really close friend who he'd like to know wasn't feeling 100 percent so he could be supportive but not romantic.

I felt the fabric on the arm of the make-out couch move, and I looked up to see who had joined me.

"So! How's it going?" Grace asked, leaning down to whisper in my ear.

"I'm so confused, Grace! He said that he was upset that I didn't tell him that I got hurt yesterday at the gym, and we were having a kissing vibe, I think, and then he stood up and said he needed a drink and left me in the dust!" I said.

"He's just nervous! Maybe he doesn't like PDA. Maybe you need to go somewhere that's more private," she said.

"What do I do? Should I wait for him to come back or go find him and ask him to go somewhere else?" I asked.

"Let's go find him!" she said. I could tell that Grace might be a little tipsy at this point, and that should have been my first sign not to follow her advice. She grabbed my hand and led me through a group of our classmates to the kitchen, where the drinks were. We scanned the crowd for an übertall kid with strawberry blond hair, but saw no one in sight.

"Maybe we missed him when he was going back to the couch?" Grace suggested.

We continued to push and shove our way through the

crowd until we made it back to the living room, where I could finally spot George and his hair, which had become his major identifying feature from afar. George was still where I left him on the make-out couch, but now he was accompanied by a girl with the shiniest, most perfectly curled black hair I'd ever seen. I froze, taking in George laugh with Elaine Lawson on the make-out couch, with George's arm resting on the back of the couch behind her. He reached up and grabbed a piece of her hair while they each started to laugh. I couldn't look away fast enough, embarrassed that I'd seen what seemed like a special moment between them.

The adrenaline from the anticipation of our kiss left my body in a gust, like someone had blown out a candle. In its place was a sense of disappointment that made my bones ache. I couldn't move with the force of it. It was one of those disappointments that confirmed your every fear that you'd somehow kept at bay with the tiniest sliver of hope. The part of me that always feared that George didn't like me back in the same way was right, and that realization hurt. Bad.

Grace came upon the scene closely after I did, and she wrapped her arm around my waist.

"Damn it, George," she whispered.

"I think I want to go home," I said, diverting my eyes from George and Elaine Lawson. Even though I wasn't looking at them, I could still picture them behind my eyes.

"You have to drive, but we can take my car," she said, handing me her keys. I was suddenly glad for Grace's driveway privilege at the party. It made for the perfect getaway car.

―――――

"Elaine Lawson? Seriously?" Grace asked for the millionth time. No matter how many times she talked about how shocked she was on the car ride home, no matter how many times she reiterated that she'd been *so sure* that we were a done deal, I did not feel any better.

When I got home, I changed into my comfiest pajamas and curled up in my bed, letting the reality of the day sink in. So. It seemed like George and I were just going to be really great friends. The reality of that sentiment weighed heavily on my chest and I felt it trickle throughout my whole body.

―――――

The next morning, when I let Fiyero out of his kennel, he acted like he hadn't seen the light of day in a decade. He took the opportunity to roll his newly groomed body all over the muddy patches in our backyard, ruining the hard work of the dog groomers who we paid a ridiculous amount of money to tame his fur every other week.

My phone buzzed incessantly in my pocket before I finally took it out to look. Of course, it was the one person I would be very content if he would leave me alone and stop sending me mixed messages, thank you very much.

George: I missed you leave last night.

George: Did you make it home all right?

George: Savannah, please answer before I send out a search party.

Well, I couldn't have him think I was stranded on the side of the road somewhere.

Me: I'm fine.

George: How did I miss you leaving? I was sitting right next to the door.

George: Parties aren't really my thing either, so I get why you would leave.

George: Why did you leave?

I tapped my phone against my forehead, trying to decide how honest I wanted to be with him. If Ashley were here, she would tell me to call him, to tell him exactly how I felt last night at the party, and be honest with him. But honesty was freaking terrifying.

Me: I didn't feel that great.

George: How are you feeling today?

George: Sorry, I'm not trying to 20 question you.

Me: Fine.

The three bubbles kept furiously bouncing up and down as he formulated his response. He must have restarted his thoughts eight times before the three dots stopped moving at all.

I shoved my phone back in my pocket, determined to forget that George had ever reached out to me. And what could be a more perfect distraction than a poodle monster who needed to burn off some morning energy?

Fiyero excitedly brought me his rope toy again and again until his tongue started to fall out of the side of his mouth in exhaustion. I knelt down to rub his belly, and he flopped down immediately.

I heard the front door slam, assuming Mom had returned from a morning run. Since we'd perfected the whole "avoiding each other at all costs" thing for the past week, I assumed that she would head up to her room without acknowledging my presence. The last thing I expected was for someone to call my name from the sliding doors.

"Savannah?" a deep male voice said, making me lift my head.

"Dad," I said. "How did you get in here?"

"Your mom gave me a key for emergencies," he said, shaking his keys for emphasis. "I finally watched the show. Thought you might need a friend in your corner."

"You're the friend Mom would be the least excited to see hanging out in my corner. I'm trying to get back in her good graces, not push it back even more," I said.

"Savannah," he said. "I drove all the way here to see you. Could you at least pretend to be excited to see me?"

I forced on a smile. "See? Super excited."

"Let's go grab a bite. My treat. We can get whatever you want, dessert, the whole shebang," he said.

I shook my head. "You can't just show up here and demand that I go hang out with you and pretend that everything is okay."

"Where is this coming from, Savannah? I thought we'd made peace with my decision to continue my relationship with Sheri. I don't understand where this hostility is coming from again," he said.

I ran my hands through my hair, fighting the urge to rip them out from my scalp. "Because. You ruined everything. For Mom."

"We hadn't been happy for a long time—"

"Stop. I'll be sick if you try to sell me that again," I said. "You breaking her heart absolutely broke her. It made me lose the mom I grew up with. What part of that don't you understand?"

For once, my father, who had an answer for everything, stood silently in my presence. He hung his head for a few moments before looking back up to the sky. Fiyero had head-butted himself in between my legs, stopping my anger from circulating around my entire body. I patted Fiyero's head, my eyes never leaving Dad's.

"I'm sorry to hear that you think that," he said.

I snorted. Of course he would try out a backhanded apology. Could he seriously have no remorse for what he put my mom through? For what he put this whole family through? Sure, I'd learned to deal with Dad and Sheri's relationship when Ashley and I lived with them while *Shake the Weight* filmed, but that didn't take away from the struggles I watched Mom go through as a result. No matter if Mom and I were fighting at the moment, I was very much on Team Mom in the whole Mom-versus-Dad debate.

"You can't tell me that after that interview aired that she's entirely happy with you," he said.

"First off, don't try to recruit me into your club of being on the outs with Mom. I will *never* be so far gone with her that she wouldn't want to see my face again. And second, they twisted my words with editing. Mom knows that. She heard the actual interview that they recorded," I said.

"I'm offering you an out. You can come hang out with me in Walcott for a bit, recuperate away from all her weight-loss stuff. I know she's tough on you about it," he said.

My mind flashed back to the desperate call to my dad a month ago, begging him to let me crash with him for a while. When he said they couldn't accommodate *guests* at the moment.

He never came through. It was like Mom and I created this little pact to hold our shit together while Ashley was gone, but now that *Shake the Weight* was taking the spotlight, our progress stopped.

"Yet, when I asked you for this same thing a month ago, you said it wouldn't be possible for me to come out and stay with you," I said.

"The timing was bad then," he said. "Sheri was just remodeling the house and starting a new job—I couldn't ask too much of her."

"You couldn't tell her that your daughter was going to come live with you for a little while?" I asked.

"It's more complicated than that, Savannah," he said. "I'm going to make the trip up to visit Ashley tonight. Do you want to ride with me?"

As much as I would love to see Ashley again, the thought of spending hours of a car ride with Dad was unbearable. I could barely look at him, let alone try to keep bubbles of silence at bay in between topics.

"I think I'm going to stay here," I said.

"Suit yourself, kiddo," he said.

Fiyero broke out from between my legs to race up to my dad. He crouched down to pet the dog, letting him kiss his face. All the memories of times we'd take Fiyero for walks around the trails in our town and the times in this backyard that Dad taught Fiyero to play fetch for the first time flooded back. Fiyero and Dad used to be best friends, especially during all the times that Ashley was out with friends and Dad took on dog duties.

He rested his face in Fiyero's fur for a moment, leaving a small kiss on his neck. My breath hitched in my throat and the lump of a bout of tears on the verge of erupting formed. Our fur baby didn't know why Dad had to leave and never came back to visit him. He couldn't understand why his best friend disappeared almost two years ago and it broke my heart that he could be confused now.

"Bye, sweetheart," Dad said, standing up and heading back toward the sliding doors.

"Bye," I managed.

After I heard the front door shut, the lock clicking in a moment of finality, I sank to the ground; I couldn't control the tears that came for what felt like an eternity. No part of me was ready to see my dad in this house again after so long, let alone seeing him interact with Fiyero. It was absolutely too much for me to handle in one day.

Two arms enveloped my entire body into theirs, and I sank into them, recognizing their hug from anywhere in the world. I hadn't heard her come home, but I didn't need to look up to realize that my mom was there, just like she always was.

"Mom," I started, wiping under my eyes.

"Shhhh, it's okay, baby," she said. "We don't need to talk about it. He's gone."

"I'm so sorry for everything," I said, my shoulders shaking with the effort of trying to hold the little pieces of myself threatening to scatter everywhere.

"It's okay, shhh," she said, rubbing my back with small circles. She alternated between stroking my hair and rubbing the comforting circles on my back, helping me calm down and find my center again. The world around me started tipping and turning less, and the anxiety attack I was on the brink of started to drift away.

She kissed the side of my head and turned me around so that I faced her. She put both of her hands on my shoulders so that we were in a deep eye contact. "Savannah. I wanted to apologize for my behavior lately. It hasn't been fair to you."

"I—" I started. "Are you sure you're okay? Mom, some of the things you've been doing lately have been pretty scary. I'm worried about you."

"Kids shouldn't worry about their parents," she said. "I'm fine, baby, I promise."

"Okay . . . If you're sure—"

"It won't ever happen again. I promise," she said.

I wanted to believe her so badly. But sometimes, even when you're reaching out with both arms to help someone, they don't see how much they need it.

chapter SIXTEEN

A note fluttered out of my locker door when I opened it Monday morning. My name was scrawled on the front in classic George handwriting. It read, *Open me, please!* on the corner of the folded paper. And one cannot ignore the demands of letters with cute handwriting.

Reasons Savannah being mad at me makes me sad:

1. I can't even look at the swings at Sandcastle Park. They remind me too much of her.
2. I can't stop checking my phone every three minutes to see if she's texted me back.
3. Not even Hawaiian pizza sounds appetizing.
4. Grace refuses to tell me what I've done wrong, even though she totally knows what I did.

5. I can't sleep knowing that I did something that upset you. Please. Talk to me.

I reread the letter at least four more times before I folded it up and put it in my back pocket. I grabbed a piece of scrap notebook paper and jotted a little something to put into his locker. It was much less well-thought-out and detailed, but it got the point across.

Make it up to me. Meet me at the Sandcastle Park swings tonight at 7.

When you leave a note like that in the locker of a boy you're romantically interested in, there is no possible way to focus on anything but that fact for the rest of the day. My mind kept playing different scenarios of moments gone horribly wrong, which prepared me in case something truly horrible did happen. But the scarier scenarios were those that I dreamed up that went in my favor. I couldn't let myself dream too much about these scenarios, to keep my heart from breaking if they didn't come true.

A little bit before seven I headed out to Sandcastle Park with Norma the Nissan. I sat inside the car for a few minutes before I started to make my trek back to the swings where George had taught me to let out my anger and frustration. I started to pump my legs and leaned back each time I rocketed forward, taking in the stars. They poked through the trees above me to say a quick hello.

I heard crunching from behind me and held my breath as George sat down on the swing beside me. I didn't dare look at him, because I had no idea what I would say. I stood up from my swing, walking over to the grassy hill that was behind us. I laid down, taking in those stars that I'd taken in just a few moments ago. George joined silently, lying down only inches away from me.

His fingers grazed mine, making fireworks shoot through my veins. I didn't dare move. What if it was an accident? What if he didn't mean to touch me? My breath caught in my throat for a few beats more before he wrapped our pinkies together.

I dared to turn my head and meet his eyes. Among the deep brown of his eyes were the smallest flecks of gold that the street light illuminated. Those beautiful eyes looked back at me inquisitively.

"What are you doing?" I whispered.

"Trying to hold your hand," he said. He scooted a tiny bit closer to me. "Do you want me to?"

I nodded; the words that I wanted to tell him were not forming in my brain. Normal Savannah would have a smart-ass comment to throw back at him, one that would make him do his classic rolling of the eyes and his secret smile. But Savannah holding George's hand? She couldn't speak, she was so thrilled.

"I like this place," he said, his eyes never leaving mine. Normally I would want to break a gaze that lasted this long, but it didn't seem strange or uncomfortable. It was George.

"I do, too," I managed. "I feel like I can be whoever I want when I'm here. Here, I don't exist."

"Do we co-not-exist now?" he asked.

"Shhhh," I said. "Don't ruin it."

He ran his thumb across the top of mine, and I gasped. I wanted to exist now. More than ever I wanted to exist in this place with him, forever. George sat up on his elbow and looked down at me, his strawberry blond curls ducking into his eyes. I reached up and pushed them away so I could look at him. My hand rested on his cheek for a few moments before I dropped it back down to my side, splayed in the blades of grass.

"Why did you leave the party without saying good-bye?" he asked.

All the fizzy fireworks dissolved inside of me, and I closed my eyes. How could I explain this without sounding like a complete weirdo? I saw him talking to another girl at the party and got mad? Even though we're not even dating? That would be a quick halt to any progress we'd just been making.

"I—I wasn't feeling that great. Dairy and I aren't the greatest combo," I said. Cute, Savannah, a lie about having a lactose attack? Very romantic.

"Sav," he said, seeing right through my BS. The way he said *Sav* sent a shiver down my spine. I wanted to reach back out and grab his cheek again.

I covered my face with my hands before I blurted out the truth.

"I saw you hanging out with Elaine Lawson at the party and thought you were into her. I got mad or jealous or whatever. I mean, it's totally cool if you like Elaine. She's really nice and pretty. And I saw you tuck her hair behind her ear. And I don't blame you, she has really great hair. I mean she must take a lot of biotin to get it that shiny—"

George pulled my hands off of my face and I looked up at him. He was inches away from me now, his fingers wrapping up in my own. My heart beat wildly and I held my breath again.

"Elaine had a hair tie stuck in her hair that I was helping her get out. That's why you left?"

"But then why did you get up from the couch?" I asked. "Things were, like, going pretty okay for us in that moment."

Even in the dark I could see Blushing George emerge.

"I didn't want our first kiss to be on a make-out couch at a house party," he said, rubbing the backs of my hands. "The only reason I went to that party was to spend time with you. I do most things now because I want to spend time with you," he said.

"Are you flunking precalc on purpose so that I stay your tutor?" I asked.

He laughed. "No, I'm actually that bad at math."

"Or I'm just a bad tutor," I said.

"Or we'd rather be doing other things than talk about math when we're together," he said.

My heart leaped into my throat. "What kind of other things?"

"These kind," he said, leaning forward.

His lips met mine softly, and I became acutely aware of the smell of him. Chap Stick and orange peels. He deepened the kiss and I wrapped my hand around his wrist, never wanting to let go.

I was in such a spectacular daze from my kiss with George that I completely forgot that I'd scheduled an interview with Chase Stevens, Mrs. Brandt's former student who played baseball, for the next morning. I looked dreamily at my phone when I woke up, expecting a cute text from George, only to find an all-caps, bold reminder to be at school by seven o'clock.

I shot out of bed and pulled on the first T-shirt I found scattered on my floor. I brushed my teeth with one hand while I combed my hair with the other before I decided that it was just going to have to be a messy-bun kind of day. On the day after my first kiss with George I would have much rather spent time to look cute, but hey, if he's still interested in me after he sees me au naturel, then I'll know he's a keeper for sure.

I double-checked that Fiyero had enough food in his bowl for the day before I ran out to Norma. There were just under five minutes left for me to get to school, and if I went ten miles per hour over the speed limit, I could just make it. Norma groaned as I tried to make her go fast automatically, but eventually she simmered down. We made it to the school with one minute to spare (and got a killer parking spot, to be honest).

I flew into Mrs. Brandt's room to find Chase sitting there on his phone. When I had tried to recall the name Chase Stevens in my mind, I'd always drawn a blank, but the moment I saw him again I recognized him. Even through the heavily smudged, fingerprint-covered trophy case, I could recognize his deep blue eyes from all of the team pictures I gazed at absentmindedly before gym class. They were piercing, really. If I were a recruiter, I would have offered him an under-the-table deal just from the power of his gaze.

"Hey!" he said, standing up and extending a hand toward me. I took it as firmly as I could manage and tried (and failed) to stop staring into his eyes.

"Hi, I'm Savannah," I said. "Sorry I'm a little bit late. Tuesdays, am I right?"

"Yeah, they're the worst," he said.

I broke off my stare for a moment to get out my recorder and notebook, setting it in between us both.

"So you were a student of Mrs. Brandt's?" I asked, pressing record on the machine.

"I was," he said. "I was actually on the *Spartan Spotlight* staff, so I was happy to come in to talk to a fellow word nerd."

A word nerd? Chase Stevens was not what I was expecting. There should be a whole chapter in my memoir called "Jocks Who I Thought Were Jerks But Are Actually Pretty Interesting." He'd be the first one I would mention.

"That's awesome," I said. "Do you mind if I just jump in with some of my questions?"

"Go for it," he said.

"So how long were you on the baseball team?" I asked.

He thought for a moment. "I was a student here from 2010 to 2014, so I was on the team starting in 2011. My sophomore year."

"And what was your experience like with Coach Triad?" I asked.

"Oh, Coach T. He was . . . you know, he's a character. But he's really good at his job. He made sure that we were as prepared as we could be for college and that we played like a cohesive team. He always said that he wouldn't tolerate divas, so we learned a lot about the power of teamwork through him," he said.

Of course he would use a term like *diva*. My skin crawled thinking back to my interview with the icky old man.

"So you never felt like he played favorites?" I asked.

"Well . . . just because he didn't want any divas on his team doesn't mean that he didn't help create some," he said.

"What do you mean by that?" I asked.

"I'm not going to call out any names or anything, but there were guys on the team who were hand-selected to be a part of this 'program' that he'd started," he said, making air quotes with his fingers. "He had friends at a lot of major colleges in the area, and they'd make face time with these people first. Like, go out to a dinner with them as a group and get to talk with them before games."

"So you weren't part of this program?" I asked.

"No, I wasn't selected," he said.

"But you still played baseball in college, correct?" I asked.

"Yeah, but I went after it on my own. It was never worth it to me to kiss his ass. And look, I think deep down he's a good guy. He has a family and kids and grandkids who come to almost every game. I'm not trying to get him fired or anything by saying this," he said.

"And what did these kids have to do to stay a part of this group? Did they have to play a certain way? Or, like, if they underperformed would they get kicked out?" I asked.

Chase tapped his fingers on the desk for a few seconds before he sighed heavily.

"You know a lot of these guys are still my good friends. I don't want any of them to look like they got an easy deal because they were part of this group. They're all good players," he said.

"But you were good enough to get into a college program without his help," I pressed. "Was he ever mad at you for not being a part of it?"

"I mean, he asked me if I would be interested, but I guess he met my mom at a practice and decided that I didn't quite fit the group demo," he said, wringing his hands.

"So is it just your mom in the picture?" I asked.

He nodded. "She's all I've ever needed. And she's all my siblings will ever need, too. I'm making sure of that now."

"So when you say that you didn't fit the group's demo, you mean . . ."

"I wasn't made of money," he said.

"Did people have to pay to be a part of this group?" I asked.

He squirmed in his seat, cracking his knuckles and avoiding my eye contact at all costs. I could see him backtracking in his mind, and I realized that I was on the brink of losing him. I went in too hot with the hard questions. Dang it, dang it, dang it.

"If you need to use a pseudonym for anonymity's sake, we totally can do that," I pushed. "No one will know it was you talking to me." I couldn't lose him yet, not when he was right on the brink of spilling some major details.

"Sure, yeah, okay," he said. He relaxed back into his seat, but I straightened up farther in mine. It was crunch time.

I leaned forward before repeating my original question. "Did people have to pay to be a part of this group?"

"Yes. People paid to be a part of this group," he said.

I wrote furiously, hoping that later I'd be able to understand my handwriting. I'd just broken a huge lead that could potentially upset the inner workings of the school system, and I had to make sure that I was getting it all down correctly. Holy jackpot, Batman.

"And where would the money go?" I asked.

"I'm assuming Triad and the recruiters pocketed it. I have no idea," he said.

"Do you think a part of it goes to the school?" I asked.

"I don't think the school would be dumb enough to get involved with it, at least not knowingly. I guess we don't know what he ends up spending the money on anyway," he said.

Holy shit. This was more than I thought I would get. And this story was going in a completely different direction than I anticipated. If I could prove that he was taking money from students to be a part of a shady recruitment ring, then my story would have the potential to get him fired.

"Do you know anyone who was a part of the group who might be willing to talk? Anyone who could easily prove that they paid him in some capacity?" I asked.

"No one who was a part of it would talk about it. They knew it was shady and it would look bad for their rep to admit to being a part of it. Recruitment is supposed to be really transparent and by the books, but this is going against all the rules that are set out," he said.

"Was there a school in particular where a lot of kids filtered into? Can you give me that much at least?"

He hesitated for a moment and leaned forward, like he

was afraid someone might overhear him. "God, if anyone figured out this was coming from me, I'd be toast. This is just between me and you, okay?"

I nodded profusely.

"I think he has a deal with the coach at Indiana Tech. A lot of them end up going there with some pretty hefty scholarships," he said. "And, I would bet that the kids who end up getting the scholarships give him a cut, since he helped make the connection. Again, this is all speculation, because I've never had it confirmed officially by anyone, but if you can prove it . . . I just want to make things fair again, especially for the kids who can't afford to pay to be a part of their exclusive group. Everyone deserves an equal chance to play in college and beyond college if they want to."

"Chase Stevens, you have just made this word nerd extremely happy," I said.

chapter SEVENTEEN

I briefed Grace on my interview immediately after and she was already writing down the ideas she had for public-records requests. There had to be one student who had been part of the club who would be willing to speak up. We were going to start with all the students who ended up going to Indiana Tech—sending them an e-mail that there was an "urgent matter concerning Coach Bill Triad"—and see if anyone took the bait. It was risky, and most of them would be smarter than to reply back, but it was worth a shot.

The anticipation of the possibility of seeing George in the hallway today was eating me up inside. I was equal parts dying to see him and not wanting to ruin our perfect night.

Grace couldn't contain her flurry of "I told you so's" when I told her every adorable detail, and for once, I was so happy to hear that phrase. George was actually interested in me as more than a friend, and I had never been more shocked or delighted.

Suddenly the prospect of homecoming in three weeks sounded less daunting with the possibility of having the best date ever. The posters that hung around the school no longer felt like they were mocking me or rubbing it in my face that I would be going alone for another year, but rather felt like a nice reminder that this year would be different. I could dress up in the all-too-frilly dress and get that pesky boutonniere that no one really knew how to put on their dates, and I could have a normal high school experience to tell embarrassing stories about when I was older.

Once the bell rang to let us out of calc, my stomach was a mess of flutters. I knew this was the time when I'd normally see George in between classes, and I could hardly wait to see his face again. The anticipation rolled over me the entire time I took my quiz, and I could not remember any of the problems that I'd just solved two minutes ago.

Grace and I made our way to the hallway, and I immediately spotted him (hair first, of course). He'd made more of an effort to comb out his hair this morning, and he wore one of his nicer Marvel superhero shirts, the one that wasn't faded and frayed from being worn so many times.

"Hey," he said as I walked up to him.

"Hey," I said back. I felt my body involuntarily leaning toward him again, almost like being within a foot of his presence meant "Welp, I guess I've gotta kiss you now." We were inches apart before he broke the tension and turned down the hallway.

"Want me to walk you to gym?" he asked, his voice suddenly tight.

So PDA was not his thing. Noted. "I want you to create a diversion so I can get out of going to gym for the day."

"What do you have in mind?" he asked.

"Wait, are you serious? Do you want to ditch?" I asked.

He shrugged. "Or we could at least go hang out in the band hall. No one ever checks in there to make sure kids are in class. We all just kind of congregate there when we don't want to go to class."

"Okay." I smiled. "What kind of tutor am I, encouraging you to skip class?"

"An extremely cool one," he said.

As we walked to the band hall I was very aware of the distance in between us. As he walked closer to me it took everything inside me to keep my hand from grasping his. I'd never wanted to read someone else's mind more in my life. Did he feel that electricity between us? Were his hands trying to launch themselves from his body and grab on to mine? I needed something, anything to confirm that this wasn't one-sided.

We walked inside the hall, and we were welcomed by an off-key symphony of students practicing in the little practice rooms dotting the hallway. There was an extremely tiny girl practicing her tuba in one room, a woodwind quartet practicing in another, and a guy playing the *Star Wars* theme on the piano just for fun in another. We went through a door at the end of the practice room hallway that led to what had to be considered their lounge. There were groups of kids sitting on a couple of old couches in one corner, but most were sprawled out on the floor working on homework. George explained that everyone gathered here for all school-sanctioned off-periods (or made-up off-periods, like us little rebels today). How did I not realize this place existed? Maybe I would have picked up the flute in elementary school if I knew that this would be waiting for me in high school.

"Welcome to the band hall, the band nerds' best-kept secret," he said.

"This is amazing," I said. "No wonder you never want to eat lunch in the cafeteria. I would totally bring mine here, too."

"It's not the prettiest space, but it's ours," he said. He led me to a spot that was open on the floor, and he pulled out a notebook. He drew a map of the music hall on his sheet of paper and showed me where each of the band cliques hung out. He reiterated that even though he was new, he fit right in with the other saxophones and stayed pretty exclusively allied with them, sometimes branching out to talk to other woodwinds. The cross woodwind and brass friendships were a little bit more strained, as they were considered the natural enemy in this setting. I loved watching the sparkle in his eye as he talked about it all, and I realized how much our time together was spent talking about me and my problems. I wanted to know so much more about him, and it excited me that this was just the beginning of that journey.

"So, this might explain some of the strange looks you're getting. It's generally frowned upon to bring outsiders into the music hall," he said.

"You're breaking some unspoken code? For little old me?" I asked.

"There are exceptions to every good rule." He smiled. Cue the melting heart. When he caught me smiling back at him, his drooped for just a second. Just enough of a falter that the same feeling I got when I thought he'd been interested in Elaine Lawson suddenly came creeping back again. Had I completely dreamed last night at Sandcastle Park? Had he changed his mind about me in the meantime?

"So how's precalc going? Need any new tutor sessions?" I asked.

"Actually I've been doing pretty well," he said, shrugging. "I think I'm finally starting to get the hang of things."

"Well, I'm happy to help, you know, considering you

took the time to learn the words to a very intricate Eminem song in my honor," I said.

He barely laughed, not even coming back with a typical retort or challenging me on suggesting that he would have just learned the words for me. I tried to search his eyes, but he was preoccupied with looking down at some random sheet music that he found on the ground. Great. Anything to avoid looking directly at me.

"You can happily report back to Hannah that I've been trying to use the Instagram theme that she suggested," I said. "Though, I'm not sure how Fiyero feels about being in a constant bluish state. He looks like a little Smurf poodle in every shot."

"I'll tell her," he said. He couldn't even riff off of Smurf poodle? That was some of my best work that he would normally be so down for.

Because I must have been a glutton for punishment, I let the question that had been bouncing around in my head all morning spill out.

"Are you thinking about going to homecoming at all?" I asked.

"I wasn't," he said. He wouldn't look up at me, and I felt like we were in the office again during the impromptu clarinet lesson, when he wanted nothing to do with me. How could it flip so suddenly?

"I mean it could be kind of fun. We'd get dressed up in ridiculous outfits and dance to terrible music, but we'd be able to make whatever we wanted out of it," I said.

He paused his doodling in the notebook, looking up at me with squinted eyes for a few seconds. I swear my heart stopped beating as I waited for his reply.

"I'm not really a dance guy," he said.

I deflated. "You're not really a dance guy, or you're not really a 'go to the dance with Savannah' guy?"

His pause was deafening. I wanted to curl in on myself. For once in my life I'd put myself out there completely with someone who I thought would reciprocate. How had I been so wrong about how we were feeling?

I stood up, leaving the lounge and all the band kids who made me feel unwelcome. Why did I let myself go down this road again? Last night was a pity kiss—a kiss to make his guilty conscious feel better about how upset I was.

"Savannah!" he called after me down the hallway.

I kept my stride, wanting to get as far away from him as possible. He caught up to me, but I pretended like I couldn't tell that he was walking in my periphery.

"Let me explain, please," he said.

"I think you've already said enough," I said.

"Savannah—"

"Please leave me alone," I said.

"Savvy," he begged.

A teacher poked his head out of the door and took us both in, eyeing me.

"Is everything all right out here?" he asked.

"Everything's fine," I said. "George was just leaving."

"Sav," he said.

"Just leaving," I repeated.

He shifted from one foot to the other for a few seconds before turning back down the hallway in the opposite direction. There was silence for a few beats before I heard the sound of George's sneakers heading off. The squeaking of his sneakers is one of those sounds that will be forever etched into my memory. The pain that I felt as I listened to his sneakers walk away was almost unbearable, and I could feel the tears that I had been holding in fall silently down my face.

I went into the bathroom and washed my face, but no matter how much cold water I splashed on it, I couldn't hide the red puffiness that came with crying. There was no way I could go back to class looking like this, and my brain was 1,000 percent not ready to focus or learn. *Damn it, George, you took away this one perfect day of school for me.*

I took out a piece of paper from my backpack and forged a note from my mom that I'd be out for the rest of the day for various doctors' appointments. The lady at the front desk didn't bat an eye at my obviously fake note and let me walk out the front of the school, no questions asked.

Norma was still waiting in her beautiful parking space so close to school. I hoped whatever latecomer for the day appreciated the perfect spot that I had cleared for them. On my way home I decided that I would shed no more tears for George. If he was going to be an insensitive ass about my feelings, then I was going to be just as callous back. I would block all communication from him. He should be happy about that—at least then he wouldn't have to pretend that he was interested in me.

When I pulled into the driveway, I cocked my head. Mom's car was still there. She should have been at work for hours by now. Maybe she called in sick? I parked on the street, just in case she'd stopped home for a second and needed to head back out.

I unlocked the front door and was not greeted by a bounding Fiyero, but I could hear him whining from somewhere inside the house.

"Mom?" I yelled as I walked in.

No response. A chill moved through my entire body. I rounded the corner into the kitchen to find Mom passed out on the floor, Fiyero resting his head next to her.

"Mom!" I yelled.

My mind seemed to work in slow motion, crouching down next to her and listening for her heartbeat. It was still beating, and I could feel her breath on my cheek.

"Come on, wake up, you're okay, wake up," I kept repeating over and over again.

I tried shaking her, hitting her cheeks, lying her on her side, but she wouldn't wake up. Somehow in the middle of this I managed to get my cell phone out and call 911. I don't remember what I said on the phone, but someone on the other end of the line assured me that they were coming.

It felt like it took the ambulance ten years to make it to our house. I sat on the kitchen floor trying everything to get her to wake back up. I even got a wet washcloth to pat along her face, but nothing was working. I begged and pleaded for her to wake up, but no matter what I said or who I prayed to, nothing about her situation changed.

I opened the door for the medics in a daze, and one of them kept asking me questions. "How long has she been out for?" *I don't know; I just got home.* "Did she come to since you've been here?" *No.* "Do you need to call your dad?" *He doesn't live with us.* The questions kept bouncing back and forth between us, but all I could pay attention to were the EMTs crowded around Mom's body. It was a flurry of activity around her until one them finally said the magic words I'd been waiting for.

"She's awake!"

I peeked over their shoulders and realized that they'd fastened a neck brace on her and put her onto one of those yellow stretchers like they had in hospital dramas. Her eyes fluttered open for the briefest moment, and it made my heart pound wildly in my chest. She was still in there.

"Mom, it's okay, I'm right here," I said.

"We're going to take her to the emergency room," one of the EMTs said. "You're welcome to ride in the ambulance with us, or you can follow along in your own car."

"I'll come with you," I said immediately. The thought of having to control a car right now was unimaginable.

I held her hand for the entire ride, never letting go. The EMTs tried to ask me other questions to distract from the fact that my mom was being taken to the emergency room, but I couldn't focus on their words. Everything was hazy and blurry around me, and the only thing that I could see clearly were our hands intertwined.

When we made it there, the EMTs helped me get out of the ambulance, and one of them told me what the next steps would be. Mom would go back to see the doctor, and they would help me find the waiting room. A doctor would come out and give me an update about her condition as soon as possible, and I could call whomever I needed to join me while I waited.

The medical team took off with her around the corner, and one of the EMTs stayed to help me find the waiting room, leading me in the opposite direction. He sat me down on the purple plastic chairs, and I became very aware of the people around me. Some of them were sleeping, some on the phone, others crying. I could not stay here alone and be okay.

I got out my phone and dialed the only person I could think of to come and meet me here.

"Dad? It's Mom. She's in the hospital. I need help."

chapter EIGHTEEN

H e made his way into the waiting room half an hour after I made the call, most definitely breaking multiple traffic laws to get there in that time. When he saw me sitting in a purple chair by myself, he raced up and wrapped me in a hug. In this moment, we forgot about the fight that had completely torn me apart this past weekend. Right now he was just my dad, the only other person who could take over the post of being strong while I crumbled.

"What's her condition? Have the doctors been back out to talk to you?" he asked.

I shook my head. "There was a doctor who said they were running some tests when she first got here, but no one has come back since. I'm supposed to stay here so they can find me when there's an update."

"Do you need something to eat? Drink? I can go grab it," he said.

I shook my head, but he went to find food. He had the

type of nervous energy where you couldn't possibly sit still. My nervous energy worked in the opposite way. I felt like I couldn't process things normally, and I couldn't get the image of Mom unconscious on the floor out of my head. What would have happened if I hadn't come home from school early? Would she have woken up and gone on with her day? Was this the first time she'd passed out like this? I had a million and one questions for her.

I went back and forth on whether it was time to call Ashley. What if they came out and said she was anemic and that she just had a really low iron count that caused her to pass out? Deep down I knew that it was something more serious than that, but holding off my call to Ashley let me hold on to the hope that it wasn't for a little bit longer.

Dad came back with a can of pop and Flamin' Hot Cheetos, and I raised my eyebrows. He'd never liked spicy food. He shrugged at me before digging farther into the bag until he had to tip the Cheeto dust at the end into his mouth. Stress is handled differently by each person, I guess.

"I'm glad you called me," he said, starting in on a bag of Doritos.

"Yeah, I'm sure," I snapped.

"Savannah," he said. "I know that we've had a rocky few weeks, but you have to know that I'm always here for you, kiddo. Whenever you need me."

"You know how empty that promise has been in the past, Dad. Don't pretend like this has always been your mantra," I said.

He set down his bag of chips and repositioned himself to be facing me head-on. "I'm trying to work on it, Savvy. My life made a complete one-eighty the moment your mom kicked me out of the house. We'd been living together since right out of college. I didn't recognize my life without her anymore."

"You made it very clear that you weren't happy in the life with her," I said.

"Neither of us was happy. And I know that's not an excuse for what I did," he said. "And that also doesn't mean that it wasn't difficult for me to adjust to a new lifestyle. To adjust to a life where my kids didn't trust me anymore."

"Weren't you the one who taught us that trust must be earned?" I asked, my voice becoming louder in my anger. I looked around the waiting room to see if anyone was watching us, but thankfully, everyone seemed to be preoccupied with their own family dramas to tune into ours.

"I did," he said. "And I still believe that. Savannah, I want to earn your trust back. I know saying this out loud won't make it magically happen, but I'm ready to put in the work."

"Savannah Alverson?" we heard from the other end of the waiting room.

When I heard my name called, I realized that this was the moment that I could no longer live in the "Mom's going to be perfectly fine" bubble. I had to face whatever reality the doctor was going to tell me now. We stood up in unison and joined the doctor at the front of the room. The walk seemed to take eons, and I couldn't complain. Right now, everything was still fine. Once he opened his mouth and told us the diagnosis, nothing would be the same again.

"Mr. Alverson?" the doctor asked. "Hi, I'm Dr. Jefferson. I met Savannah earlier."

We both nodded in unison.

"I have some good and bad news for you both. The good news is she was breathing the entire time she was passed out, so there's no sign of brain or organ damage. The bad news is, her blood work is showing that she is severely malnourished and has been effectively starving herself. We've put a call into our adult psychiatry unit that specializes in mood and eating disorders to see if there is a bed available for her. When patients come into my office with these signs and they are no longer able to make their own choices, we admit them," he said.

"So . . . what does that mean? How does this transition happen? When does it happen?" Dad asked. All his questions blurred together in my head. From the moment the doctor said the words *starving herself*, I completely shut off. I'd seen it—I'd seen how different she was acting, and I didn't do anything about it. I could have prevented this all from happening. She wouldn't have to be in the hospital if I had said something earlier.

"We'll keep her here for as long as we can and hope that a bed opens up within our own adult psychiatry unit. If not, we'll put feelers out to units in the area until we can find a place for her to stay. In cases like these, it's a two-week minimum stay with limited visiting hours in the first week. I'll be able to give you more information once we know which facility she'll be moved to," he said.

Dr. Jefferson rested his hand on my shoulder and my head sank. Dad continued to ask the doctor more questions, but I couldn't focus on the words coming out of either of their mouths. I squeezed my eyes shut, hoping that when I opened them back up this would be a terrible nightmare. But I was still surrounded by plastic purple chairs and sad people as far as the eye could see.

Dad thought that we should start calling family at this point, and he volunteered to call most of them. I insisted that I call Ashley, but I started sending him phone numbers of everyone else I thought might need to know.

I decided to take my call with Ashley outside, where the birds still chirped and the sun shined down on me. If someone had told me when I scrambled out of bed this morning that I'd end up calling my sister with really terrible news about our mom, I wouldn't have believed them. But here I was, terrible news and all.

She picked up on the third ring. "Hey, Sissy! What's up?"

"Ash, it's Mom," I said, my voice cracking.

"What happened?"

"I came home from school early, long story, and found her passed out on the kitchen floor and couldn't wake her up. The paramedics had to come and take her to the emergency room."

"Oh my God."

"We just heard from the doctor that she's going to have to be admitted to a mood and eating-disorder facility because she'd been starving herself," I said.

She was silent for a few seconds on the other end of the line, I'm sure she was trying to figure out her route home and how to clean up this uncleanable mess. She didn't have a car up at school, so either someone was going to have to come get her or she was going to have to find a Greyhound that came back this way.

"I'm going to see if I can borrow Yael's car for a few days and make my way back home. I should be there by tonight. Are you there alone?" she asked.

"Dad's here with me. He's calling the rest of the family who I feel like need to know," I said.

"Thank God for Dad," she said. "Stay strong, Sissy. I know this is awful, but everything will work out. It always does."

"It's kind of hard to believe that right now," I said.

"Just keep remembering that I will be there soon and it won't all be on you anymore. I'll be there as soon as I can," she said.

Our loved ones started piling into the hospital waiting room an hour after we started our phone train. Grace came first, and she sat beside me, holding my hand until the doctors would come out with more updates. They had been able to find an open bed within the hospital's psychiatry unit and they were admitting her as an eating-disorder patient. They weren't sure how to classify it yet, but based on her lab results and her extreme weight loss, they were confident that she should be admitted to that unit.

I'd been instructed to go home and grab a few things that she might need—a toothbrush, pajamas, a pillow— anything that you might bring to a sleepover. They did make one special request: no objects with sharp edges. Grace drove me home and helped me assemble the bag. We let Fiyero outside for a bit, but he kept looking around the house for Mom. I wished I could bring him with, even if it was just for a few minutes, to show him that she was okay. I knew he was worried about her, and it broke my heart that

I had no idea how long he'd been trying to wake her up before I got there.

Ashley did end up borrowing Yael's car, and she was already waiting in the hospital when I got back with the bag of things. She enveloped me in the biggest hug humanly possible, and I clung to her for relief. I knew that I would be able to get through whatever was thrown at me with my sister by my side now.

We gave the bag of her things to the nurse who was helping facilitate Mom's transition, and she told us that we'd be able to see her tomorrow morning. She gave us directions to get to the unit and told us to check in with the front desk so they could let us in. It hit me then that she would be locked in this place with no way out. It would be so that she could heal and recover, but it felt very scary and final in that moment.

Ashley and I piled into Yael's car and headed back home to let Fiyero out and attempt to sleep until we could see Mom again in the morning. Dad was close behind in his own car. We didn't speak as we drove home, but I appreciated the silence. I'd been talking to people all day, reliving the horror that was finding my own mother unconscious on the floor, and I was ready to stop having to explain myself.

The house felt emptier than ever when we walked in. Fiyero tackled Ashley to the floor when he saw her, and I pretended not to hear her crying. She had been trying hard to be so strong for me this whole day, but I think it had all finally hit her in this moment. I went to the fridge and picked up a cup of yogurt. I hadn't eaten all day, so I knew my body was hungry, but the thought of eating food right now made my stomach roil.

I sat quietly for a few moments, the only sound coming from my spoon hitting the bottom of the yogurt container. Ashley's footsteps sounded up the stairs, followed by a fluffy poodle monster who was going to be incredibly happy to have his bed buddy back again.

In this moment I felt the most exhausted that I ever had in my entire life. I slunk up the stairs and collapsed onto my bed, too tired to even move the covers or take off my shoes.

It had to be an hour later when I woke up to the feeling of someone removing my shoes. My eyes fluttered open to find my dad standing at the end of my bed. He had a blanket in his hands and he was laying it on top of me. He paused when he noticed my eyes were open.

"Keep sleeping, kiddo," he said.

I held out my arms to him and he fell into a hug, bringing me closer to him. I didn't dare let go, because if I did, he might disappear. "Thank you for coming."

"Oh, sweetheart," he said. He hugged me tighter as I started to cry. I didn't know how many times I'd imagined that he was back in this room reading me a bedtime story or telling me a silly joke before I went to school in the morning. I missed this part of him that I'd shut out so firmly when I found out that he cheated on Mom. It had taken me this long to realize that even if they didn't love each other anymore, it didn't mean that he didn't love me still.

Eventually I drifted off to sleep while he sat on the edge of my bed, drawing comforting circles on my back. That night I dreamed of the last time we took a trip as a family to California. We were all walking along the beach and picking up seashells when Dad pushed Ashley into the ocean, and I doubled over I was laughing so hard. She pretended to be angry, but she couldn't help but laugh herself. Even Mom was joining in on the fun. I remember thinking in that moment that it was perfect, that it was my idea of complete happiness. Dream-Me took a seat on the beach, watching the rest of the scene play out. It no longer made me sad that this memory was the last one of us being happy as a family. Because now I realized there was a possibility of making new happy memories with both Mom and Dad, and even if the memories weren't made together, eventually they would bring me just as much joy as this one did.

chapter NINETEEN

D ad stayed with me for the first two weeks that Mom was in the hospital. We'd convinced Ashley that it was time for her to go back to school only three days after Mom was first admitted to the psychiatry unit, no matter how many times Ashley insisted on staying. I ended up being the only one allowed to visit Mom once Ashley was gone, and Mom was still pretty angry about her situation. Though I think she was starting to understand that she was there for her own good. It was taking her time to realize that her brain had been working against her for many years.

I sat on the end of her bed the day that marked the end of her mandatory two weeks, and we played a mean game of Chinese checkers. It had always been one of my favorite games to play with her growing up, and I could remember the pride I felt the first time I beat her at a game. It was still unclear if she'd let me win on purpose.

"Has Dr. Brenneman told you when you'll be ready to be discharged yet?" I asked.

She placed a marble in the perfect spot to start a train into my corner, and I looked around, trying to find a way to sabotage it. Darn it! She was too good.

"Ha!" she exclaimed, hopping her marble down the train until it landed at the point of my star. "He thinks it will probably be another two weeks of inpatient, then I'll be coming back for regular checkups. He said that if I'm progressing it could be earlier, but I want to make sure that I've had as much care as possible. I want to be in good shape for when I get to go back home with my girl."

"Take all the time you need. I think you're doing amazing, and it's a huge step that you want to stay here and get help," I said. Plus, I think Dad was having a new real bonding moment with Fiyero. They were fast best friends again.

"It makes me feel terrible that you've been having to spend so much time here when you should be spending your time enjoying your senior year. I just want you to have normal-kid experiences," she said.

"I'm still having normal experiences," I said. "Remember that story that Grace and I were working on? Well, it turns out our baseball program is totally doing some shady, under-the-table recruiting with colleges. The story ran on Monday and Mrs. Brandt submitted it to this national high school newspaper competition to see if we can win anything for it."

"What part of that sentence was a normal high school experience?" she said. She tapped my foot with her own. "How did I raise such a smart kid? I can't believe you came up with something like that."

"I'm doing other normal high school things," I said. "I'm going to homecoming with Grace and her boyfriend. And I'm going to go with his friend who still needed a date."

"Well, that will be fun. He's a nice boy, isn't he? I need to see some pictures, please," she said. I looked up Cole Yen's Facebook page to show Mom his picture, and she made little comments like "Has a good chin," and "We'll have to tame that cowlick before we take pictures." Hearing her talk like that, like her old self, made me feel warm and safe. I felt like I was getting to know my mom again for the first time, and I loved the person who I was getting to know more than I ever could have imagined.

"Grace and I are going dress shopping after school tomorrow. She's convinced that I need to get something pink, since she'll be wearing orange and they will comple-ment each other. I don't know how I feel about pink, though," I said, crinkling my nose.

"You'll be lovely in pink," she said. "Your hair and your

complexion will suit it. I hope you wear your hair down in luscious curls. You have the most beautiful hair."

Her compliments made me gasp. It had been so long since she'd said anything positive to me about my physical appearance, so long that I couldn't remember the last time that she said something that made me feel good about how I looked.

"I'll be sure to send you pictures of all my options," I said.

"I'm sorry I couldn't take you shopping," she said, taking my hair in her hands and starting to braid it. "Moms are supposed to take their babies dress shopping for every special occasion."

"We still have prom," I said.

She kissed my cheek. "That's my positive girl."

As far as best friends went, I think Grace had to go down in the history of most supportive ever. In the past two weeks, she'd done everything in her power to support me and distract me when necessary, including taking me dress shopping for homecoming. She'd dropped all her plans with Ben for the past two weeks to put me first, which was totally unnecessary, but I was beyond grateful to have her around during this difficult time. She'd even called ahead to make sure that the stores we ended up going to carried my size of dresses, which took off another level of stress from my plate. There's nothing more frustrating than going to a store and not being able to dress your body in the adorable clothes on the rack.

We ended up going to a boutique dress shop in town that advertised great deals for women of all sizes, and we marveled at the dress selection when we walked inside. There were dresses up to size 30 available in-store, and dresses that started at size 2. Having the ability to shop at the same store with my best friend was such a blessing, and I didn't have to feel like a burden for asking to go to a store that only I could specifically fit into.

"Hi! I made an appointment for Grace Moreno?" Grace asked at the front desk. The girl at the counter smiled at us and checked a name off a list before picking up a phone.

"Laura? Your two-fifteen is here for you," she said, turning to us. "Laura will be up in a second to help you both out."

"Thanks!" Grace said, already eyeing a sherbet-orange dress to her left. Grace had been perfecting her spray-tan regimen to fulfill her dream of a creamsicle-esque dress. Not that she needed to tan much, with her naturally olive-colored skin.

"Isn't this just divine?" she said, holding up the long, flowing dress in front of her. It was. Her long legs could fill out the floor-length skirt, where as if I wore it, I would need at least six inches taken off to not be drowning in fabric. My goal today was to find a short dress that looked as if it was made for a fun-size, five-foot-tall human.

"It's great," I said. "Perfect color—it totally suits you."

"You think?" she asked.

"I know," I said.

"Grace?" someone said from behind us. We turned around to find who I assumed to be Laura, the sales associate who was helping us find our dream dresses today. She wore a metallic body-con dress and the coolest patchwork heels that I would kill to wear. You know how I roll—the more color, the better.

"Hi!" Grace said, coming up to her with the creamsicle dress still in hand. "You must be Laura. This is Savvy."

"Nice to meet you both! So . . . What's your vision for homecoming? Have you been eyeing anything in particular?" she asked.

Grace held out her orange dress. "Something like this. I really want to make orange work for this year."

"Good, I like a plan. What about you, Savvy?" she asked.

"I really have no idea," I said. "Maybe something that will look good in photos with Grace's dress?" I said.

"I love a fresh palette," Laura said, rubbing her hands together mischievously. "We're going to try a bunch of different types of dresses on you until you find one that you like. Are you up for that?"

"Yes," I said. It actually kind of excited me, the prospect of someone helping me find my perfect dress.

We told Laura our dress sizes, and we followed her around the store as she pulled dresses for us. A few of the dresses made me shake my head in protest, but she insisted that they would look beautiful on. Since she was the expert, I trusted her opinion.

I walked into the dressing room, where all the flouncy dresses in various bright colors and patterns screamed out to me to try them on. But, for some reason, a pink two-piece dress kept catching my eye. It had delicate velvet roses embroidered on the top piece, and a baby-pink tulle skirt to match. The top had cap sleeves and was cropped so a part of my stomach would peek out between the top and skirt.

I pulled the rose-covered top on over my head and admired how the pink complemented my hair color. It was less vibrant than I would normally go, but the understated nature of it made me feel like a princess. I pulled the ballerina skirt on next and gasped as I twirled around. It didn't look too long, and it hit me just at the top of my knees. I could imagine the perfect pair of lilac heels to accent the embroidered flowers on the top, and the flower crown that

I could fashion out of my hair. It all seemed to come together in my head.

. "Let's see it, Savvy!" I heard Grace yell from outside the dressing room.

When I walked out, both Laura and Grace gasped, and that was all the confirmation I needed. It wasn't just me who thought this was the most gorgeous dress ever.

"Oh, Sav, it's so pretty," Grace said. "I know you're not normally a light-pink girl, but it looks so great."

"Damn, I wish this style would have been in fashion when I went to homecoming," Laura said. "Girl, you could wear that skirt and top with separate outfits after homecoming. It's, like, the most versatile thing ever."

"It's not too much with my stomach showing?" I asked.

"Absolutely not," Laura said. "I see that smile on your face. I know how you felt when you looked in that mirror. You look gorgeous, you feel gorgeous, so wear the dress."

I looked at myself in the mirror one last time before I turned back to both of them.

"Okay. I've found the most perfect dress in existence."

———

Grace and I were instructed to come into Mrs. Brandt's room early the next morning, so she picked me up at 8:00 a.m. sharp.

"What do you think is going on?" she asked. "Do you think the school is mad about our story?"

"The school is most definitely mad about our story," I said. "But I don't think she would call us in early to state the obvious."

"So you think this has to do with the competition?" she asked.

"My new mantra is stay cautiously optimistic, so I'm being cautiously optimistic in thinking that it's about the competition," I said.

She turned up the radio and we had a stoplight dance party in (cautiously optimistic) celebration over our story placing in the writing competition. The parking lot was virtually empty, so we got another killer spot in the front of the school. If I didn't hate waking up so much in the morning, I would get here this early just to avoid having to deal with the parking lot.

When we walked inside the door, Mrs. Brandt let off a small confetti cannon, which scared the living daylights out of me. Grace and I both clung to each other until we realized that there was confetti raining down on us from Mrs. Brandt's desk.

"Oh my goodness, that was a lot more alarming than I thought it would be," she said. I brushed the confetti off the top of my head as she came to stand in front of us, her hands behind her back. "I'm so happy to announce . . . that you two have been chosen as finalists for the Indiana Student Journalism Association's in-depth-reporting competition! You've been invited to attend their convention next month, where they will announce the winners."

"Oh my gosh, this is amazing!" Grace said. We each took a pamphlet from Mrs. Brandt's hand with our official invitation resting on top. It read that there would be journalism professors brought in from across the country looking for students who might be interested in their programs.

"So you'll think about going?" Mrs. Brandt asked.

"We'll more than think about it," I said. "Consider me signed up."

Grace bounced as we left the room, and her excited energy totally rubbed off on me. I couldn't contain the smile that crept on my face. I'd never been so invested in a project or worked so hard on it in my life, and to have it recognized on a large scale was overwhelming and thrilling.

Possibly just thrilling enough to lead me to a future that no longer involved Indiana State's engineering program.

chapter TWENTY

Dad insisted on coming along to Ben's house to take pictures of me for homecoming, and even though I pretended to be very embarrassed, it felt magical having him there. Especially since Mom couldn't be. I felt like I was really living out a normal teenage moment, and everything else that might be so not normal about me disappeared for the night.

Cole was a perfect gentleman the whole night, even when I accidentally stabbed him in the chest with the boutonniere pin. Thankfully, someone's mom had a Tide to Go pen to get the tiny bloodstain out of his nice shirt.

We piled into Ben's car, and I tried my best not to buckle up the excessive amounts of tulle from my skirt. Dad waved at me from the front door, and I waved back. He mouthed for me to "be safe," and I mouthed back, "Love you."

Ben drove us to the Marriot downtown, which had transformed one if its ballrooms into our "Evening of Stars" homecoming. Gold, glittery stars hung down from the ceiling, and plastic glow-in-the-dark stars were scattered all over the dance floor. It was the perfect level of cheesy.

Grace wrapped her arm around my waist and pulled me in to her.

"I'm so glad you came," she said.

"Me too," I said.

"How are you doing, Savvy?" she asked. Her question held more weight than just a quick check-in. She knew how badly I wanted to come here with George, and how guilty I felt worrying about boy drama when my family drama was so much more important at this time. She knew I was a big flurry of confusing feelings that I could hardly wrap my own mind around, let alone share with another person.

Since she knew all that already, I lied.

"I'm doing okay, really." I smiled. It didn't quite reach my eyes.

"It's okay to admit that he hurt your heart," she said. "It might take a while to get past it. But I swear you will. Who knows, maybe you'll be head over heels with Cole by the end of the night. That's the beauty of being seventeen—you aren't tied to one person forever."

"I just feel so silly being upset about it with all the stuff going on with my mom," I said.

"Just because you're going through some family shit

doesn't mean that your feelings turn off in the meantime. And it sucks, because that's what you want to focus all your energy on, but it's not something you can switch on and off. It might take time. But it *will* get easier," she said.

I wrapped her in a big hug before dragging her out onto the dance floor. Ben and Cole joined us, and I found out that Cole was actually a pretty good dancer. We did some school-dance classics like the "Cupid Shuffle" and the "Cha-Cha Slide," and Cole even danced with me for some of the slow songs. He was an A-plus perfect date, and I was so glad that Grace had talked me into coming.

As the festivities wound down and the homecoming king and queen made their final rounds on the dance floor, our group decided it was time to head out. Our next destination was Ben's basement, where we'd play video games and eat junk food until we all passed out. The boys walked out first to the car, and Grace and I were close behind, replaying a moment on the dance floor, when Ben dropped it low and just about ripped his pants.

We both stopped dead in our tracks as we took in George standing in the middle of the parking lot. His hands were in his pockets and he shrugged at me, a silent plea for me to talk to him. Grace started her angry walk toward him, but I grabbed her arm.

"I've got this," I said.

"Are you sure?" she asked. I nodded, and she looked in between us, her eyes resting on George's for a few beats. I like to imagine that she sent him a warning through their telepathic cousin bond.

I approached him slowly, being extra careful not to trip in my high heels. I knew that I should have practiced walking in these more. When our eyes met, I forgot about all the disappointment and hurt that I'd felt because of him. All I could see now were the beautiful moments we shared together in Sandcastle Park. I wanted more of those beautiful moments desperately.

"So." I stared at him, the silence hanging between us. He was still looking at the ground, at my abnormally fancy feet cramped and uncomfortable in the heels Grace convinced me to wear. I suddenly felt ridiculous for painting my nails a sparkly pink.

"I'm sorry that I didn't agree to come to the dance with you in the first place," he said.

"Don't apologize," I said, tapping my feet. "It was weird of me for being so upset about it. Of course you didn't want to go to the dance—it's not your scene. I get that now. I'm sorry I flipped."

He sighed heavily, looking up at the stars. Here we go. Here comes the speech where he tells me that he's not interested in me the same way that I am. That I was right, but he was too much of a coward to admit it when I first asked. The pre-rejection bumblebees in my belly stirred and stung as I waited for him to speak again.

"Can we go somewhere to talk?" he asked.

"Whatever you have to say to me you can say here," I said, crossing my arms.

"Savannah, please," he begged, his voice almost a whisper. The bees that had turned in my stomach froze along with my heart. Something was wrong. I nodded, following him to his mom's Jeep that he'd been able to borrow for the night.

"Fine. Let me go tell Grace that I'm headed out with you," I said.

My hands were shaking as I approached Grace, who had a stern look on her face. I'd never seen her go into protective mode like this, but she was definitely not happy to see her cousin in this moment.

"I'm going to go talk with George for a minute. You guys go ahead, I'll have him drop me off at Ben's later," I said.

"Are you sure?" she asked, resting both of her hands on my shoulders. "We're having a fun night. I don't want him to ruin this memory for you."

"It'll be fine, Grace," I said. Maybe if I put that sentiment out into the universe it would be true.

"If you're sure," she said. "Text me if anything goes wrong, and we'll come get you. Promise me you'll text?"

"I promise," I said. She pulled me into a tight hug, and I could only imagine the glare she was sending to her cousin. A good tip to everyone ever: don't get on Grace Moreno's bad side.

My lilac heels made a loud clomping sound as I approached George again, and I tried my best to emulate Grace's stern face. I walked past him as I approached him and went straight to the passenger's side of his car.

He drove in silence, and I started to unpin my hair from its fancy updo, sighing in relief as the pins unhinged themselves from my scalp. Bobby pins were the work of the devil himself.

I recognized the trail into Sandcastle Park from a mile away. Was he taking me back to my spot to let me down? He was not allowed to ruin this for me. Absolutely not.

Our feet crunched in the grass and my footsteps quickly matched up to my hammering heartbeats. My heartbeat pulsed through my entire body, and the old saying "The anticipation might kill me" had never been more true. He motioned for me to join him on the ground. I tucked the ridiculous pink tulle under my legs, but it still fanned out around me, creating a five-foot radius around us in every direction.

"Savannah, I haven't been completely honest with you," he said.

"What do you mean?" I asked. How I managed to form a coherent sentence while simultaneously holding my breath seriously beats me.

"I did want to take you to the dance. I want to do everything with you. I just—I'm scared," he said.

"What are you scared of?" I asked.

He put his head in his hands, taking a few beats to find the words that seemed to swim around his mind, just out of reach. I put my hand on his shoulder, and he leaned into it, lifting his eyes to meet mine again.

"I've never felt this way about anyone before. You were all I could think about, and that night when we were at the party, when I figured out that you'd been hurt and I didn't know . . . It made my stomach sick thinking that I did nothing to make you feel better. It scared me how in such a short amount of time, you'd become this integral part of my life.

"And then it scared me even more to think about you leaving for college next year, especially whenever you'd talk about how hard it was having Ashley away at school. I don't know if I could bear getting even closer to you knowing that it all might end in nine months. And then I felt ridiculous for thinking of an *us* nine months from now because we're only sixteen and seventeen and—"

I grabbed his hands, like he had grabbed mine the other time we were in this alcove together. The last time that we'd had such a monumental miscommunication because of our fear of how much we truly liked each other.

"Why didn't you just tell me that?" I asked. "I was so convinced that I had been making this all up in my head, that there was no possible way a guy like you could like a girl like me."

His eyes blinked open, dumbfounded. "What do you mean? It's me who should have been worried. You're so smart and driven and funny—what were you doing wasting your time with me? If you haven't realized yet, I think you're pretty rad. And there's no one on the planet I'd rather spend every second with more than you."

"Well, that's good," I said, taking his hand, "because as far as people on this planet go, you're pretty high up on my list, too."

He squeezed my hand. "I didn't freak you out, did I?"

"No way," I said. "You could say pretty much anything to me at this point and I would still be obsessed with you. You know you're one of my favorite humans, right?"

He nodded. "Same here."

"Right now, I'm super content hanging out with George, my more-than-friend who I occasionally kiss. Let's not get freaked out by the future, and let's just enjoy what we have right now. Because nine months is a *lot* of time," I said.

"I don't want to hold you back," he said. "I don't want to influence your decision on where you go to college, because you deserve to go somewhere wonderful, even if it's not close to Springdale."

"I am happy *now* here with you, just as we are. I'm not worried about what might or might not change in the future. I want to be here, with you now, in our favorite place to co-not-exist. We deserve to let ourselves be happy now."

He cupped my face in his and pressed the sweetest kiss to my lips, and I had never felt more connected to another person in my life.

epilogue

Mom was being discharged on the same day that Grace and I were making our big adventure to the Indiana State Journalism Convention, so Ashley came up to make sure that everything was sorted. Dad booked a hotel room down the street for the next week while Mom got back on her feet around the house. I made sure that everything was clean and that Fiyero went to the groomers the day before she'd be back so that he was the most handsome boy around when she got to see him again.

I'd definitely overpacked for the convention, not sure if I should be rocking a blazer-and-skirt combo, or if people would be more business-casual throughout the whole weekend. Grace had done a bit of due diligence stalking the Facebook page from last year's convention, but the outfits seemed to be a mixed bag. I'd prepare for whichever scenario seemed to present itself when we got there.

I shoved one last blazer in my suitcase before I heard the

honking of Mrs. Brandt's car in the driveway. Mrs. Brandt would be the chillest chaperone ever, and I couldn't wait to start the journey with her and Grace to the convention.

"Kick some ass, superstar!" Ashley yelled behind me.

I blew her a kiss as I got inside. Mrs. Brandt used her GPS that she'd programmed to have an Australian accent, and we laughed each time it interrupted our songs to tell us a new direction. Thank goodness we were on this trip together. I don't know that I could have handled a convention of reporters without them.

Our top convention priorities included a panel with a reporter from CNN who Grace had a professional crush on, a class on producing the news with just your iPhone, and, of course, the awards ceremony. We'd already prepared ourselves to gracefully accept defeat if our article didn't end up winning. We'd even practiced our "I'm so happy you won" faces to flash at the team that does win. I felt like we were heading to our equivalent of the Oscars.

When we made it to the fancy convention hotel, we marveled at the height of the ceiling and the exposed elevators that took you up to the tippy top. Mrs. Brandt went to the front desk and returned to us with two room keys.

"I'll be just down the hall from you ladies, if you need anything," she said, handing me the card. "But you have some free time to explore the convention center while I go to a teachers' orientation. Want to meet in the lobby after your first panel?"

"Sounds good!" we said in unison.

Our room was on the tenth floor, and we hopped into one of the space elevators that rocketed us up at top speed. We watched all our fellow high school word nerds check in and explore the hotel from above, and it really started to sink in that we'd be spending the whole weekend with like-minded students. That, and complimentary hotel breakfast. Both were pretty exciting prospects.

Grace beeped us into our room that looked just as fancy as the lobby. When you walked inside, you could see a big whirlpool bathtub and floor-to-ceiling mirrors that would be perfect for checking out our morning outfits. We could properly assess our blazer-skirt combos every morning.

"We're living like queens this weekend!" Grace exclaimed, flopping onto the bed.

"Queens who have to share a full bed," I grumbled.

"At least the school decided to send us. They still aren't too happy about the article, and the whole 'having to open an investigation against Coach Triad' thing," she said.

"Semantics, shemantics," I said. "I still think it's cool that we get to be here."

"It's definitely cool. And if we want to get good seats at

that CNN panel, we need to leave now. I must have front-row seats for Instagram opportunities!" she exclaimed.

We made it in plenty of time, beating out most of the other students by a long shot. Grace got her Insta-worthy shot of the reporter, and we continued on to different classes and workshops throughout the day. My nerves started to build as we got closer to the awards ceremony, until it was the last ten minutes of our last workshop and the nerves escalated to peak anxiety.

My phone buzzed and I looked down to see George's name flashing.

George: No matter what happens I'm super proud of you. Don't be too nervous!

I smiled, bringing my phone into my chest. How was it possible that we'd only known each other for a little over three months but I felt like he knew me better than myself? He had quickly become the one person I can tell everything, completely unfiltered, and always have it received without any judgment.

The master of ceremonies called the awards to order, and I snapped my attention up from my phone. It was go time. I purposefully kept my expectations low so that if we didn't end up winning I wouldn't be completely heartbroken. But when they got to our category, my palms dripped with sweat, which I wiped down my pant legs.

I could barely focus on what the presenter was saying when he explained what qualified people to enter the investigative-reporting category. Grace gripped my hand fiercely, and I thought she might cut off my circulation.

"In second place . . . Merrill High School for their story on refugee families in their town," the announcer said.

I held my breath as he took out the envelope for first place. *You might not win. You might not win, and it will still be okay. You might not—*

"Springdale High School for their story about unethical recruitment practices in their high school baseball program," the announcer said.

"That's us!" Grace yelped. We shuffled our way to the front of the stage and shook hands with the announcer. First-place medals were placed around our necks, and Grace and I couldn't help but flash giddy smiles at each other. We'd done it. After so many interviews and so many hours doing research and making public-records requests, we won.

After all the award winners were announced, we were invited to a mixer with the students, speakers, and representatives from different colleges at the convention. Networking wasn't normally my scene, but I felt like I could strike up a conversation with anyone while I had that medal around my neck.

A woman in a suit-dress combo started walking my way, and I put on a big smile for her. She reached her hand out and I took it.

"Hi, Savannah, I've been dying to talk to you," she said.

"Hi!" I said, feeling my whole body flush at the thought of someone wanting to seek me out.

"My name is Marlene Jenson, and I'm with the journalism department at the University of Missouri. Mizzou is known for its stellar journalism program, and we're always looking for students who have a gift for reporting. Ever since I read your story as a judge, I knew I had to keep my eye on you."

"Oh, thank you! I'm so flattered," I said.

"Trust me, the irony of my 'recruiting' you from your story about illegal recruitment is not lost on me. But here's my information anyway," she said, holding out a crisp business card. "I can't promise any under-the-table scholarships, but if you have the right grades, there might be money available for you here. Just something to think about."

"Thank you," I said, taking the card. "I definitely will think about it."

By the end of the night I had cards from five more schools who had sought me out. They each had a slightly different pitch about why their journalism school was the best and, honestly, they all sounded wonderful. Going to any school that took reporting seriously and wanted to continue on the tradition of responsible media sounded like a dream to me.

When we got back to the hotel room I wanted nothing more than to call George and tell him all about the win and about all the cards I'd gotten. Grace was already wrapping herself up in the bed cocoon-style, and I looked at her sheepishly.

"Do you care if I call—"

"Fine, fine, go be lovebirds. But do it quietly. I need some beauty rest," she said.

I snuck off into the bathroom and perched myself on the counter, resting my feet near the sink. The phone rang twice before he picked up.

"So, what's the verdict?" he said.

"We won," I said.

He started playing a recording of "Who Let the Dogs Out" and I had to hold my mouth to keep from cackling. It was so random, but the most wonderful celebration song that I ever could have asked for.

"I knew you guys would," he said. "Take that, Merrill! This really is your Oscars moment. You beat Merrill!"

"Ha!" I burst out laughing. Grace groaned from inside the room and I vaguely heard "shut up" mixed in with it.

"And then after the ceremony I ended up talking to about five journalism advisers from different schools around the country. *They* came to find *me*. How wild is that?"

"Again, I'm not surprised," he said. "You and Grace obviously put a lot of time and effort into that story, and it shows. I mean, you got that old perv put on indefinite leave. Not every student group in the school has the power to expose a horrible teacher for who they truly are. And only a fraction of the people in that group has the guts to pursue it. I'd say you're pretty incredible."

"You are playing out your role as my official hype man spectacularly well," I said. He laughed on the other end of the line. "But truly, thank you for helping me believe in myself. I sometimes need the extra boost."

"And I'm always happy to boost. You should get some rest—I know you have more to do tomorrow," he said.

"Yes, and then I'll be home again with Mom and Ashley. Things are finally going to go back to normal," I said.

"You deserve some normalcy," he said.

"That I do."

ACKNOWLEDGMENTS

I have to give it up again to the big two in my life, my parents, Heather and Rich Martin, for their unwavering support in everything I do. I am incredibly lucky to have been born into your family, and I thank the universe and the cosmos every day for that gift.

Endless thanks to my little sister, Abbie, for everything you've taught me about being a decent and loving human. I'm proud to call you my sister and my best friend.

One of my favorite characters in this book ended up being the beloved poodle monster, Fiyero, who is 1,000 percent based on my dog, Scooter. He has shown me what love an animal can bring into a family and has made me a complete animal lover. (He's getting a longer paragraph than my parents, that's how obsessed I am with him.)

To my grandpa Mike Harrington (SwoonPa, as he was so lovingly called by the Swoon Reads staff when we visited

Swoon HQ), for everything. You are a rock star. To my grandma Judy Harrington, thank you for giving me my love of reading (and I did it again! A green cover!).

Also to the leader of our Martin clan, my grandmother Kathleen Martin. You paved the way for an amazing family. (Hi, Martins!)

This book would not have been possible without the *amazing* vision of my editor, Emily Settle. Thank you for always being my number one fan. And to the rest of the team at Swoon Reads, I'm forever indebted to your tireless work. Thank you, Jean Feiwel, Lauren Scobell, Ashley Woodfolk, Teresa Ferraiolo, Morgan Rath, and Carol Ly. (I will forever remember the happy tears I cried when I got the first e-mail with cover concepts.)

To the Swoon Squad for being the best group of support that any author could ask for. Special shout-outs to Jennifer Honeybourn, Lydia Albano, Alex Evansley, Olivia Hinebaugh, and Katy Upperman for the extra support. You have all been so impactful on my journey as an author.

To my friends who constantly support me behind the scenes in ways I'll always be grateful for: Matthew Nagorzanski, Stephanie Tabor, Talya Miller, Stormy Smith, Allie Windergerst, Jorge Hernandez, Catherine Orr, Matt Cooper, Larissa Wilming (photographer extraordinaire!),

Jessica Batastini, Kaitlin Wilkerson, Will Pruyn, Tay Ross, Laura Bucklin, Sydney Johnson, Caitlin Enlow, Jess Peterson, and someone I'm sure I'm forgetting (please don't hate me).

But most of all, this book is for a younger Maggie who I wish could see herself for how truly beautiful, inside and out, she was. I think she'd be pretty proud.